Found Mysteries:

The Rebirth of Violet Franklin and Other Tales

Three Novellas by Nicholas Westbrook

The Death of Venus Harlow

Bryce

Bryce had yet to meet a ghost who was genuinely pleased with their demise, timely or not. Since his tenth birthday, ghosts would come to him at all hours asking for help. As he got older, Bryce learned the biggest problem with being the only medium for miles around was that he heard everyone's complaints.

"My sister buried me in the wrong dress."

"I still haven't beaten Larry Olsen at cards, and I lost $700 to that bum!"

"I was just getting milk..."

Some things couldn't be fixed. A ghost from the Victorian Era plagued Bryce for months demanding revenge for her murder. In the end, the spirit only left Bryce alone when he drove her across the state to see her killer's gravestone. Bryce had been tried for identity theft after trying to donate a deceased couple's fortune. Once, the ghost of a woman asked him to sue the car company that had been responsible for her death, but Bryce had been laughed out of enough courtrooms. He preferred the requests that were to deliver messages or forgive someone, even if families rarely enjoyed his presence. To Bryce, the living and the dead were intolerable. He did his best not to get too personal with jobs. The less invested he was, the faster his jobs went.

However, Venus caught his attention. Curly brown hair framed the sides of her face, and she had a narrow nose and a slightly gapped smile between broad lips. She was still wearing a lab coat from the pharmacy where she worked, though it seemed dingier than any medical professional could bear. And, while he thought she was cute, that wasn't the reason he chose to help her.

It was how she'd asked that got his attention. The sadness in her voice was a mix of regret and loss, almost like she was blaming herself. Her smile was bitter with the thought that she was somehow guilty.

"I don't remember much..."

"People usually don't," Bryce said. "I've met ghosts who don't even realize they're dead. Some spirits are so traumatized that they block it out and keep trying to go about their lives, ignoring—sorry, I didn't mean to interrupt."

"No, it's fine. Anyways, I was walking through town at night—I know, I know…single girl, shouldn't be walking around alone, blah, blah, blah. I had just popped out to grab a burger on my way home from the late shift at the pharmacy."

"Where'd you get the burger?" Bryce asked, taking out his pen.

"Rocket Burgers on Market Street."

"I prefer Benjamin's on 9th."

Venus shook her head and recoiled. "They drench the bun in mayo and it feels like chewing a sponge. Besides, they're the only place I've seen with a C health rating."

"They may have a C in health, but an A in price and taste. I can live with a B average. Please, continue."

"Anyways," Venus took a deep breath, "I was walking back, munching on a few fries. Everything was fine until I was waiting to cross the street. Something happened that made everything go black. When I came to, I was laying in the street. I barely got to my feet before a bus went straight through me. Or…I went through it? I don't know the terminology."

"Either is fine," Bryce said. "Though I've never considered it. The grammar of intangibility is tricky. So, you were on Market and….?"

"5th, I think. My legs kinda go on autopilot when I'm listening to my headphones."

"You were walking around wearing headphones after dark?"

"I know, I know…" Venus sighed, dramatically falling back in her chair. "I learned my lesson and only hope others learn from my demise."

"Alright, so you wake up and then what?"

"Right, wake up, the bus does the—" Venus made a quick swing with her right hand, "*whoosh* thing and I stagger back onto the sidewalk. I tried stopping people, but they couldn't see me. After that, the first guy who saw me told me to come see you."

"5th and Market. Skinny guy? Big, bushy beard?"

"That's the one!"

"Okay, okay…" Bryce made a note. "One more good deed I'll have to thank Connor for. Do you wanna find the guy who killed you?"

"At the very least, I'd like to know my murder was reported."

"We can see about that pretty easily," Bryce said, picking up his phone and dialing Clay's number. "One perk of being a popular medium is a familiarity with police, whether they like it or not."

Bryce looked up at the ceiling while he waited for someone to pick up. His brain was already working on the details of Venus's case and picking out the important facts. The phone stopped ringing and Detective Clay picked up the line.

"What do you want, asshole?" Clay grumbled. "I've got a stack of cases I'm working on."

"Clay, you know I didn't call just to hear your cheerful voice. I need a favor."

"No way! I'm already the laughing stock of the precinct by listening to the guy who talks to ghosts."

"The guy who talks to ghosts and helped you close a three-month murder investigation over two days. Come on, do me a solid. I just wanna check on a murder."

"Fine!" Clay grunted. "You don't get a consultant's fee unless I ask for your help, by the way."

"I need you to see about a Venus Harlow. H-A-R-L-O-W."

"And Venus like the Greek goddess?"

"Roman."

"Just say 'yes' next time. Harlow…Harlow…nope, nothing in homicide."

"Well, I've got her sitting right in front of me."

"For Christ's sake, Bryce, don't try drumming up business without evidence. Do the superstitious old women on your block not want to know who their son is going to marry?"

"I'm a medium, not a psychic," Bryce said. "They don't like when I step on their toes. I'm telling you, she's sitting right in front of me and I need to know if it's been reported."

"Fine. Nothing in homicide, but the name did come up in the missing person department. I'd be all too happy to throw you over to them and let you bother someone else."

"Nah, no need for that. How long has she been missing?"

"Roommate called it in first thing this morning. Happy?"

"Ecstatic," Bryce said, dryly. "How long would it take to move her into homicide?"

"We don't just push cases around like playing cards, Bryce!" Clay caught his volume and dropped his voice. "I can't just say that a ghost whisperer told me that someone was dead and not missing. You want her case moved to homicide? Get me a body."

"Can you give the roommate's address?"

"Hell no! I'm not giving you a civilian address. Ask your ghost friend."

"Always a pleasure, Clay."

"Stop calling me, Bryce."

Bryce ended the call and set his phone aside. "Okay, good news and bad news."

"They don't know I'm dead?" Venus asked.

"No, I'm sorry. The good news is that your roommate came looking for you this morning. Still just a missing person case, but that means I have somewhere to start."

"So, you'll take my case?"

"I can't promise an arrest, but the police need to know you're more than a missing person. I won't say murder yet, but I think we can find out what happened."

"What's first?"

"Step one is the roommate. She already knows you're missing, maybe she'll know more if I ask the right questions."

On a cold night, Venus Harlow was murdered. It wasn't what she'd wanted.

Venus had hoped she would finally meet her end in one of two ways: doing something heroic or in her sleep when she was much older. Ending up a ghost after going out for fast food didn't strike her as something that would get a statue erected in the city park. She might get a bench or a plaque somewhere if her parents could find the money. Overall, she'd rather still be alive.

The strange thing to Venus was that she didn't feel dead. She had expected death to be sore and painful, like the time she'd had the flu as a child and could barely leave her bed. Truthfully, she felt fine. It wasn't until her encounter with the bus that she felt something was wrong. She'd tried talking to other people on the street, but no one acknowledged her. Dejected, Venus sat on the curb while people walked right by her on their way to work.

"Lost?" a gruff voice asked. The question made Venus jump and fall into the street again. Staring down at her was a rail-thin man with a thick beard and broken glasses. His eyes were rimmed with dark circles and his lips were too thin for the rest of his mouth. The stranger chuckled a little and leaned against the lamppost. "Everyone struggles on their first day, don't worry."

"First day?" Venus asked.

The man extended a hand to Venus and smiled. "Call me Connor, your guide to the world of ghosts."

Venus reached out and took Connor's cold hand. To her surprise, he helped her to her feet. It was a small comfort, Venus supposed. It felt better having a name for what she was going through, even it meant —

"Wait, I'm dead?" Venus asked, her jaw dropping.

"You're quick!" Connor grinned. "That'll make finding your rest easier."

"My what?"

"Anyone who's a ghost has unfinished business. That's the tricky part of it. Personally, I'm a coward and I'm too scared to pass on. I help Bryce out in the meantime. So, what about you? Got a gambling problem?"

"No."

"Drugs? Unrequited love? What about a lost child?"

"No, no, and definitely not."

"How about hidden money you never told anyone about?"

"I just got out of grad school! If I had buried treasure, I would have spent it."

"Ah, murder then! That's a real shame, my condolences. However, I know just the guy for the job! Come on!"

Connor led Venus through the city, not bothering to stop for crosswalks and letting vehicles pass through him. Venus still checked both ways before crossing and had to run to keep up. Connor pushed on through the city, only pausing when Venus struggled to follow him through the back wall of a Chinese restaurant.

"Focus on your intent," Connor coached her, standing with his head poking out through the brick wall. "You just wanna take a few big steps forward. Don't think about the wall. This is Introductory Ghosting, so I'd feel guilty leaving you without knowing the basics."

It had taken a few tries, but Venus eventually figured it out. It was a strange feeling, like pushing against a strong current of water, but Venus was quick to pick up the ability. Connor and Venus passed through a few more walls until Venus was more confident. Before she could ask to learn more, Connor stopped in front of an apartment building.

"This is where I leave you," Connor said. He pointed up at a big, brick building with blue trim around the windows. "Third floor, at the end of the hall on the right. Follow the sign. Rest assured, you're in good hands. I wish you the best."

"You're not coming up?" Venus asked.

"You wouldn't want me sticking around. Bryce's work tends to get kind of personal, whether you realize it or not. Best of luck." Connor bowed deeply, smiled, and stepped away from the curb. After watching him pass through bustling traffic, Venus turned back to the building and marched up the stoop.

Closing her eyes, Venus strode through the front door and foyer. Venus opened her eyes and followed Connor's directions until she found the door marked *'Bryce Dell: Medium. Ghosts enter to left'.* Confused, Venus took a big step to her left and walked through the wall into Bryce's office.

Bryce was not what she had expected. Venus had expected an old charlatan with a crystal ball or chalkboard weaving a tale for people who were too good-natured to challenge him at his word. However, his office in the apartment was just a desk, a couch and a few succulents on the window. The desk had an Ouija board on it, but the laptop Bryce was typing on neutralized the mystical air. A small hallway connected to a kitchenette and a closed door that Venus guessed was a bedroom. Bryce waited at his desk, watching Venus as she walked through the wall into his office. A man in his late-twenties, Bryce had a bit of gut and thick black hair. Bryce introduced himself and was nothing but genuine when he invited Venus to sit down and tell her story.

After talking with Bryce and having him call the detective, Venus was relieved they finally had a direction to go. Bryce didn't have a car, so they left for her apartment on foot. It was comforting to have someone to talk to. Connor had been nice, but treated Venus more like a naive student. When no one was nearby, Bryce would talk to Venus like she was a real person.

"You worked at a pharmacy?"

"Just measuring out prescriptions for now. I got my Master's a few months ago. Since then, I've been applying to doctorate programs."

"Impressive! I barely finished high school. You come to the city for your Masters?"

"Came for school, stayed for work while I was figuring out what came next. My folks are from — oh, shit!"

"What?"

"They have no idea." Venus paused on the street and dropped her shoulders. Bryce walked a few more steps but waited for Venus to collect herself. "They don't know I'm dead. We have to call them! They need to know I'm — "

"Let me stop you there," Bryce said. "I don't drop the news. That's too high above my pay grade. If there was a disagreement you wanted to get squared away, that's one thing. But I don't break the bad news…too many emotions. I only talk to families if they know you're already dead."

"Not even if the ghosts are kids?"

"Kid ghosts are rare," Bruce said, walking again. Venus had to walk much faster to keep up with his quicker pace. "When they do come up, I make that Clay's job. When your family 'gift' is seen as a shame and they write you off as a liar and a thief? Let's just say I've spent enough time in handcuffs to stop knocking on parents' doors."

"I can't imagine," Venus said, looking down at her toes. "It must be very lonely."

"You kidding?" Bryce asked, cracking a grin. "I have ghosts walking through my door once or twice a week. I would love to take a vacation, but I'm always working!"

Venus smiled back and looked around her old neighborhood. Things seemed a little brighter now and she felt comfortable with Bryce. They weren't rushing towards a solution, but Venus figured that any progress was a better place to be than when she woke up earlier today. They'd find her killer.

No. She'd find peace. Venus didn't need to find blame. She just wanted this all to be over.

Bryce pressed the buzzer impatiently. He'd already pushed the call button about three times, but the remaining occupant of Apartment C3 didn't answer. The old brick building was on the corner across from a rundown bar and a three-chair barbershop. Ivy vines were crawling up from the soft dirt by the concrete stoop and stretched up to the first floor windows. It had charm, but the chipping paint on the doorframe made Bryce wonder if the building was properly cared for.

"Why do I still feel cold?" Venus asked, rubbing her forearms. "I mean, I don't have a body anymore. That means no nerves, no skin, no muscle. Still, I feel cold. Am I supposed to feel it?"

"It's your mind telling you what to feel," Bryce explained. "You see the leaves, the wind, the overcast sky. Your brain says 'Autumn'. You see I'm wearing a coat and look down at your thin sleeves. With all that, the conscious part of your essence tells you that you're cold."

"Mind over matter?" Venus asked. "That's not very scientific."

"You asked," Bryce shrugged. "I'm a medium, not a ghost. That's how Connor explained it to me once. Are you sure she's home?"

"It's Tuesday. The diner always gives Amanda Tuesdays and Thursdays off. I'd think she'd be home eventually."

"Could you go and check?" Bryce asked. "I'm not a fan of B and E, but it's technically your home, too."

"The door's—oh, right."

"Mind over matter," Bryce nodded, tapping his temple. "Don't rush it. I've seen ghosts accidentally drop through floors to the basement if they weren't focusing."

Venus took a deep breath and stretched out her hand against the door. The wood resisted her passing through, but Bryce figured Venus was still learning. She wasn't at the level of some ghosts he'd met, but she was a quick study. After about a minute of pushing against the door, Venus passed through. Bryce leaned against the doorframe, put his hands in his pockets and waited.

"Can I help you?"

Bryce turned and saw another young woman approaching the stairs. She had pink, shoulder length hair, round eyes and a stack of posters in her hands. Bryce saw Venus's smiling face on the poster.

"Are you Amanda Williams?" Bryce asked. "Venus's roommate?"

"Did you know her?"

"We're new friends," Bryce explained. "Can we have this conversation inside?"

Amanda looked him over, carefully. "I have a taser in my purse."

"Blunt transition, but I accept your terms." Bryce motioned to the door and stepped aside. Reluctantly, Amanda walked up the stairs and unlocked the door for him.

"How did you and Venus meet?" Amanda asked as they walked up the staircase to the right of the door. "I'm assuming you weren't dating?"

"Because she didn't mention me?"

"Venus didn't date. She wasn't interested in a romantic relationship. Mom would say she was 'Career Driven,' but she was just content with her platonic relationships. Aromantic, I think she called it. Perfectly fine roommate, but happy enough on her own."

"Live and let live, I always say," Bryce smirked at his joke. When they approached the door to C3, he had to stifle a yelp when he saw the bottom half of Venus's torso sticking out the door. Amanda couldn't see anything out of the ordinary and opened the door.

Closing the door behind him, Bryce looked down at a very annoyed Venus with her arms folded across her chest.

"I messed up and my legs got stuck," Venus grumbled. "Mind over matter…this isn't as easy as you think!"

Bryce rolled his eyes and followed Amanda into the small apartment. To the left was a short hallway with two doors to the left that must have been the bedrooms. To Bryce's right, Amanda was setting the missing person posters down on the kitchen counter and digging through her purse.

Pulling a small device from her bag, Amanda slapped her taser on the table. "Hope you don't mind. I prefer to show I'm not bluffing."

"You don't strike me as the bluffing type." Bryce raised his hands and carefully put them flat against the table. He'd been in this situation before. Amanda watched him for a minute. Bryce guessed she was sizing him up, trying to figure out exactly what kind of person he was. He'd been on this end of an analysis before: parents, cops, family friends. Amanda's intensity was stronger than any of those. She was looking at him as more than a medium. Whether she saw him as a suspect or ally, Bryce guessed even Amanda wasn't sure.

"Water?" Amanda offered, keeping her defenses up.

"I'm fine, thank you."

"What do you know about Venus?" Amanda asked, sitting across from him with a hand loosely on the taser.

"She's been missing since last night, as far as you know."

"As far as I know?"

"I'm, uh—" Bryce slowly reached into his coat pocket with two fingers and took out a business card. "I'm a medium. Been a police contact for a few years, go on ghost hunts with professionals, and do private consulting pro bono for spirits from time to time."

"A pro bono medium?" Amanda picked up his card.

"Hard to send debt collectors after the dead."

"Prove it," Amanda said. "What's something Venus told me that only we would know? Who was my first kiss?"

"Bobby Jacobs," Venus said from the doorway, still trying to free her legs. "She thought he was ugly, but then he got really hot after they broke up in eighth-grade. She regretted not staying with him through to high school."

"Your eighth-grade boyfriend, Bobby Jacobs. You wished you'd stayed with him until high school."

"Okay, how about the first *girl* I kissed?"

"Cindy," Bryce relayed the story Venus told him. "After you and Venus had gotten drunk at a bar, you met Cindy at a taco place. You two came back here and—"

"Okay, okay!" Amanda cut him off. "You made your point. Is…is Venus here?"

Bryce looked back towards the door as Venus finally pulled her foot through the apartment door. "She is."

"What happened?" Amanda asked.

"She's not sure," Bryce said. "That's why she came to me. You turned in a missing person's report, but they can't investigate it as a homicide until they find her body. That's where I come in, nudging the police in the right direction."

"You think someone killed her?" Amanda asked, keeping her expression still.

"That's what I'm hoping you can help me figure out. How did you know Venus was missing? It's been less than eight hours, from what I know."

"Venus worked too much, but she was consistent. Her Monday night shift always ended at seven, then she'd grab something to eat, and would have been home by eight at the latest. She never made it back. She didn't answer any of my texts and all my phone calls went to voice mail. Venus isn't one to make other people worry."

"Did Venus have any—and I use the term as much as it can be applied to a twenty-something pharmacist—enemies?"

"Enemies?" Amanda asked. "Not really. There were a few guys who didn't appreciate when she rejected their romantic proposals, but they usually got over it. She was polite and a classic Midwestern girl, ya know? Every 'please' and 'thank you' that should muster in one breath. She had some issues with another classmate or two in her graduate program, but no one with enough malice to kill her, if that's your question. She was just kind of a know-it-all."

"I resent that!" Venus folded her arms and paced around the table. Bryce's eyes followed her and Amanda turned to follow his gaze. She looked back at Bryce and he cleared his throat with a cough.

"Where were you when she went missing?"

"Here," Amanda gestured around the apartment. "I was streaming a micro-concert for my subscribers. Pays the bills quicker than trying to land a contract."

"Besides you, did Venus have anyone else in her life?"

"She has a big family, but most of them are on the other side of the country. I called her dad before I got in touch with the police. He hadn't heard anything from her, but he can't do anything from where he is."

"Any other friends?"

"A couple of coworkers, but not really. Venus was a pretty content person. More often than not, she'd spend nights in her room applying for schools or watching TV. She'd come to my shows, but that was about as social as she usually got."

"Anyone you didn't know about? Secret boyfriend or platonic partner?"

"No way. Venus couldn't keep a secret if her life—" Amanda's smile faded as quickly as it came. "Sorry. It just comes rushing back into focus and startles me. To think she's actually…gone."

"Not gone," Venus said, sitting next to her at the table. Venus reached out to put a hand on Amanda's forearm, but her fingers passed through. Amanda shivered a bit and touched her where Venus had tried to touch her.

"Will you find out what happened?" Amanda asked, her voice quivering. "I can't pay you, but—"

"I'm pro bono for things like this," Bryce said. "I want to make sure she gets her rest."

"Can you tell her something for me?" Amanda asked.

"She's right next to you. She can still hear you."

"It feels stupid."

"It's not."

Amanda looked to her right, but Bryce knew she was only looking there because that's where he had pointed. "Vee? I want you to know that I'm still looking. You may have Captain Specter over here, but I'm still looking for you. I'm not gonna stop until I get to the bottom of this, I swear."

Amanda frowned and pushed her face into the crook of her palm. Venus smiled a little and looked up at Bryce. She reached for Amanda's shoulder, but stopped and folded her hands on the table's surface.

"She says, 'thank you,'" Bryce told Amanda. "I'll show myself out."

"Can I fly?" Venus asked, walking with Bryce. "I always thought ghosts could fly."

"Well, gravity requires mass," Bryce explained. "Technically, since you don't have any mass, gravity doesn't influence you. It's your mind telling your form to stay on the ground because that's all you know. Once you get the hang of it, you can glide or even levitate. But fly? No."

"Cool!" Venus nearly sidestepped a street sign, but decided to phase through it instead.

"You're getting better."

"Practice makes perfect," Venus said. "How long until I can make people see me? Non-mediums, I mean…"

"The people you know? Decades. Strangers? Centuries. However, I hope to have you well on your way before that."

"Couldn't I stay?" Venus asked. "It's not so scary anymore and some of this ghost stuff is kinda fun!"

"It gets less fun," Bryce said. "Not everyone who dies stays as a ghost. Eventually, you'll lose so many people that you'll go mad. It's bad to die, but when the rest of the world you know moves on — and it will — grief will break you. It's why so few ghosts like to have reasonable conversations. By the time most can vocalize to strangers, they're too far gone. The spirits of this world are meant to pass on, not stay. Death is natural. Eternity on Earth? That's suffering."

Venus quietly walked beside Bryce, hands in the pockets of her lab coat. She looked down and focused on the toes of her shoes as they came into her line of vision. It was hard for her not to imagine everyone leaving her for the afterlife that she was missing. The feeling clawed at her belly over a loss that hadn't even occurred. Venus was startled when Bryce paused and looked up at the intersection of 5th Avenue and Market Street.

"This is where our investigation starts," Bryce said, taking a few pictures of the street corner on his cellphone. "So…you're killed here, fall into this bus lane, die by the time you hit the ground. What happened next?"

"I got up and—"

"Not for you," Bryce said. "This place is clean as a whistle. No body, no blood, nothing. Street cleaners must have passed through before you were even reported missing. Either you have terrible luck or we're dealing with someone with a lot of experience. Since your spirit started here, it means your body was moved somewhere after the act."

Bryce examined the sidewalk and looked around. "Wouldn't want to use the crosswalk with a dead body over my shoulders. Heading down 5th leads to too many restaurants and people. Your killer probably took your body this way on Market."

"Are you sure this is legal?" Venus asked, timidly trailing behind Bryce as he walked down the street. "Shouldn't we call your cop friend?"

"Technically, we're still on public property," Bryce said. "We can examine the sidewalks and alleys, but if we want to enter a building or something, that needs a warrant. Anyone asks, I'll just pretend I'm a photographer or something."

"I guess. Shouldn't I be where my body is?"

"Not necessarily," Bryce said. "Otherwise, we'd have a lot more ghosts in graveyards. Ghosts normally stay where their trauma occurred…like a big fire or a murder. It can have very strong emotional connections and they would rather feel something."

Bryce paused suddenly and turned a corner into one of the smaller alleys. He stood with his back to a dumpster and put his hands in his coat pockets. "Take a peek."

"What?" Venus asked.

"In the dumpster," Bryce elaborated, taking out his phone and scrolling through some texts. "It's the closest place to drop a corpse."

"Ew! No, I'm not going in there!"

"Look, just pretend you're on a beach. You don't have a nose anymore, so you can't even really smell. Just block it out."

"You sure?" Venus grimaced.

"Yeah, just take a quick peek. If this guy was a professional, this is the closest place to get rid of a body. If we find it, we'll tip off Clay and—ta-da! You have your rest and I get back to my regular life."

"But a dumpster? It's so…cliche."

"You're probably right, but murderers don't care about originality. Come on, quit complaining."

Venus cringed, took a deep breath, and plunged her head through the top of the dumpster up to her her neck. Inside the dumpster, it felt like a swamp or a too hot summer day. After a few seconds, she came back out, retching and gagging. "It smells awful in there! I thought you said I couldn't smell?"

"You're still thinking that you can smell." Bryce shrugged. "Did you see anything?"

"No, I was too busy trying not to throw up!"

"Throw up what? You don't have a stomach. Take another look."

"Really?" Venus groaned. "No! That was absolutely disgusting!"

"There's a lock on it, so I can't go in. However, you can pass through without a warrant. You're not paying me, so think of this as your contribution. It's faster this way."

"Okay, fine," Venus cringed. She took a deep breath and pushed her head back into the container. The imagined odor filled her nostrils and she could only pretend it didn't bother her for a few more seconds. Venus pulled her head out of the container with a gasp and coughed a few times. Through watery eyes, Venus saw Bryce chuckling at his phone."You're enjoying this, aren't you?"

"Probably more than I should," Bryce admitted. "Come on, keep your eyes focused in there."

"They're gonna make fun of me, aren't they?" Venus whined, sitting on the big leather chair in Bryce's apartment. "All the other ghosts and ghost hunters from around the country will get together and swap stories about me. I wonder what they'll call me. The Garbage Ghost? The Smelly Spirit?"

"The Putrid Poltergeist?" Bryce mustered a grin, hanging his coat on the hook by his door. "Sorry, I couldn't resist."

"Easy for you to say," Venus sneered. "You weren't the one sticking your head in dumpsters all day. And we didn't even find anything!"

"I admit, the endeavor was fruitless, but the good news is that we don't have to go check the dump. Trash day is tomorrow."

"Well, there's that. Can you turn on the shower for me? It may not do anything, but I want to trick my brain into think I don't reek like garbage."

"Mind over matter," Bryce said, going into the small bathroom. Twisting a knob, Bryce made sure the water coming out of the head was still fairly warm. Venus thanked him and passed through the curtain.

Bryce sat at his desk and opened his computer. He wasn't a cop, but he liked to pretend he could think like one. The fact remained that he didn't have much to go on. Bryce sat at his desk and made a few notes in the document he kept open for Venus and frowned. Apart from what the roommate had told him and an unsuccessful day of dumpster diving, he had nothing.

It felt too organized, too clean. The person responsible didn't want to get caught and they were far too efficient for this to be a crime of passion. Bryce didn't think it was premeditated. Venus was too kind for a bullseye on her back.

Still, kindness didn't protect Venus. Bryce needed help. He didn't know enough ghosts to ask for their help and Connor would have said if he saw anything. Bryce could ask the traffic center if their cameras had seen anything, but that would have already been reported to the police. Venus's killer was going to be harder to catch than Bryce had thought.

The vibrating phone made Bryce jump. He answered it quickly and held it to his ear. "What's good, Clay?"

"Hey," Clay whispered, "I probably shouldn't say anything, but I think you'll want to know this. Someone came into the station tonight in response to finding a missing person poster—"

"You can't blame me for those. The roommate put those up before she talked to me."

"I don't care. Listen, someone said that they saw a person who matched your so-called ghost's description the other night. He thought that she was drunk college girl getting driven home by her boyfriend or something."

"Coming or going?"

"Coming. The witness says he saw her brought into a big apartment complex on the corner of Luther and Pine. It's called Willow Grove Apartments."

"Great, send in the troops!" Bryce said. "You really should be talking to someone higher up the ranks than your typical, dime-store medium."

"Except that the judge doesn't see proper cause yet. A hazy tip about a missing person isn't enough to search an entire apartment complex. We're trying to get through the red tape, but the landlord assures us nothing suspicious is going on in his building."

"So, you want me to investigate?"

"Don't get excited. You're not above the badge, but if you go in, poke around and find something? That'd be enough to get us inside. We can do the rest if you can get us a picture of something: blood, something she was wearing—a body would be best."

"Undercover work, great. Where's my cyanide pill if I get captured?"

"You're on your own for that one. Not that I hate putting you in handcuffs, but you'll have to be careful."

"You're welcome, dick." Bryce hung up and dropped his phone on the table.

"Who was that?" Venus asked, walking out of the bathroom. She was still wearing her pharmacist's coat, but it looked fresher than before.

"Clay said someone recognized you from the posters. Did you ever visit Willow Grove Apartments? Over on Luther Street?"

"Not especially. There's a bar or two out there that I've been to with Amanda, but I don't know anyone who lives in that part of town."

"It's a bit off the beaten path, but Clay thinks it's worth having a look around. Someone matching your description was taken inside that building."

"So…whoever killed me took my body home?"

"That seems the most likely, yes."

"What kind of—?"

"I'm less concerned about their thought process," Bryce explained. "I just want to find who killed you. The police can handle the why and how."

"What's the plan?"

"I am going to email the building manager to get myself a tour. We can use that as cover for you to poke around to see what you can find. I hope your more confident walking through walls than you were walking through Amanda's door."

"You're interested in the two bed, one bath?" The landlord, Tom, asked. Tom was tall man in his fifties with broad shoulders and a completely shaved head.

"Wife and I are looking for a new place." Bryce shrugged. "She's looking for a space to use as a home office or potentially a room for a future Bryce Jr."

"Yikes, this is hard to listen to," Venus said. As Bryce continued talking with Tom, Venus walked through the hallway. While Bryce was keeping the landlord busy, Venus would have to go into each room to find some evidence of her killer. Bryce said she might have an hour before he had to leave.

At this time of day, most people were already at work, but Venus could still find traces of human life in each room she walked into. More than once, Venus encounter a cat or dog that would stare at her as she passed through a family's space. She raised her hands in apology when the animal disapproved of her presence, but she kept moving forward. Strangely, the walls were easier to pass through than doors, so Venus spent little time in the hallways. She only got stuck a couple of times and didn't waste a lot of time in each room.

Once the first floor was cleared, Venus continued on to the second floor. Halfway through her search, she suddenly felt sick to her stomach. As she walked through a wall, the apartment seemed to lurch and her head spun. It took her a few minutes to regain her balance. Something about the room made her sick. She hadn't experienced anything like this since dying, so she knew that it was significant. The closest that Venus could remember feeling this way was when she had her appendix burst right after she graduated high school.

The only way Venus could describe it was that the room felt 'wrong.' It wasn't one particular factor. What scared Venus most was that it looked so normal, but she felt worse the further she walked around the one-bedroom apartment. There were a few dishes in the sink, some art from a sci-fi show Venus hadn't seen and a sprawling spider plant by the window. No matter where she looked, her stomach felt like it was being clawed at from the inside. She had to get out.

Venus ran straight to the door in a panic. Doors were so ingrained in her habit that she tried grabbing the doorknob three times before forcing herself through the door. She twisted and pushed against the wood, desperate for every inch that she could gain through the wood. Her head and shoulders got through easily, but it felt like the room was holding her feet as she tried to pull her hips through. Venus kicked and flailed until she was nearly out up to her knees. Finally, one foot came loose and Venus desperately pulled at her trapped leg before it came free. She collapsed on the floor and scrambled. Venus stared and took a few breaths in the hallway. She felt more like herself, but the knot in her stomach still weighed her down.

"—should let you know in a few days," Bryce said, stomping down the stairs. "I'll do my best to get the wife out here. That bedroom has an amazing view."

"I do have others interested in the space."

"Naturally." Bryce glanced down the hall and met Venus's gaze. Venus desperately pointed at the door number, nearly jumping up and down. Bryce covered the glance with an exhale and a nod. "I'll talk to the lady of the house and get back to you tomorrow?"

"Sounds like a plan." Tom smiled and shook Bryce's hand. "Let me walk you out."

Once back on the street, Venus walked next to Bryce, talking excitedly. "Something was wrong with that place. I haven't felt anything that weird since dying."

"What do you mean by weird?"

"In the pit of my stomach…I could feel it. I was sick and disoriented. That has to mean something, right?"

"Could mean a few things," Bryce scratched his chin. "There could have been something to do with your murder in there. You could also have been a negative connection to whoever lives there…or worse."

"What's worse than the person who killed me?"

"Some violent spirits will terrorize other ghosts until they're powerful enough to effect the living. And if we're dealing with a professional killer, there are bound to be a few violent skeletons in his closet."

"Didn't think to check there. What's the plan, partner?"

"Well, you have some connection to that place. I'll put in a call to Clay and see what he has to offer. If you can connect it to a name, maybe I can convince Clay to visit."

Bryce held his phone to his ear and stopped to lean against a wall in a side alley. "Clay? It's Bryce—yeah, I know you said not to call, but if we can connect an apartment to Venus would that be enough to get you a warrant? Willow Grove, right. Apartment B6. Yeah, yeah, yeah, I owe you big time. Just hurry up…"

There was a long pause. Bryce shifted uneasily on his feet while Venus paced back and forth. Bryce leaned forward and whispered to Venus. "Fredrick Wood? Mean anything to you?"

Fred had been Venus's classmate in her graduate school program. They had more than the friendly animosity that comes between peers, though Venus wondered if it was really as friendly as she thought. Fred would glare at her when she answered a question he didn't know the answer to and refused to work with her in labs. Venus wasn't sure Fred truly hated her enough to make her feel like his apartment had made her feel.

"Venus?" Bryce asked again, a little firmer.

"I, uh…Fred was someone in my graduate class. I'd always thought it was just a healthy rivalry."

"Clay? Venus and Fred had some beef in college—"

"Grad school."

"—and there might be something there. Call it a hunch or an anonymous tip, but would that be enough to search the room. Okay. Yeah, I know. Later, Clay."

Bryce hung up his phone and slipped it into his pocket. "Clay's gonna try the legal route. Good work today."

Few people could sleep with a ghost in their apartment. Venus had curled up in the large, leather chair and didn't respond when Bryce announced he was going to bed. He'd left the TV on for her. It was hard falling asleep to the noise, but it was easier than having a discontent spirit wandering into his bedroom.

His sleep had been restless. Bryce felt like he'd barely crawled into bed and closed his eyes when his phone started to buzz on his nightstand. Bryce cursed a few times before answering.

"What?"

"Your lead was a bust."

"Clay?" Bryce grunted. "It's the middle of the night."

"It's almost six in the morning."

"If the sun's not up, I consider it night." Bryce sat up and turned on the lamp by his bed. "What happened?"

"Your lead was no good. Judge says we don't have enough for a warrant. Fred's got a clean record aside from a few parking tickets."

"Does he have an alibi?"

"He was working a shift at the drug store with three other people on the night you said Venus died. They all confirmed he was there. It's a dead end."

"I'm telling you, Clay, there's something about that building."

"Well, if I go to my supervisor again with another one of your 'feelings'? This case is gonna lose momentum. More than a day of that and I can guarantee that this goes cold. The missing person department isn't happy that I'm sticking my hands in their business."

"Alright," Bryce said. "I'll figure it out."

"You better," Clay said. "I'm sticking my neck on the line for you and you owe me big time."

"I said I'll figure it out!" Bryce barked and hung up his phone. He fell back on his bed with a sigh.

"That didn't sound good."

Bruce jumped up, startled. Venus was standing in his doorway, though he didn't remember her coming in. She could have been standing there all night, for all he knew. Venus's hair was still the same and her coat was still clean, but Bryce could see the dark circles under her eyes. Her skin looked a little paler and her irises were starting to lose color. If there was anything Bryce liked about ghosts, it was that it was easy to read their emotions.

"Hey, Venus. Sorry, but Fred has a solid alibi working on the night you were murdered. Sad to say, you just really got under his skin."

Venus slumped and sat on the bed. The mattress bent a little under her form and Bryce nearly forgot she was a ghost for a moment. He would have liked to reach out and comfort her, but it would have felt forced even if he could touch her. "I'm sorry, Venus."

"I just want this to be over. I want to sleep. Heaven, Elysium, Valhalla, Reincarnation…whatever's on the other side is preferable to walking through walls and feeling so hopeless. This ghost stuff is starting to get less fun."

"I know, but I got a good feeling about that building. I can stall for a bit longer and try to get more time in the building."

"How?"

Bryce rubbed his chin and exhaled. "I think I can enlist some help.

"Thanks again for doing this," Bryce said. "There's no way to ask about it that isn't weird."

"I appreciate being in the loop," Amanda smiled. "I just wanted to help and you're not tricking me back to your apartment. Plus, I still have my pepper spray."

Venus walked behind them, never far from Bryce's view. Venus was quiet with her hands in her pockets. She'd almost joined the conversation once or twice, until she remembered that Amanda wouldn't hear her anyways.

"So, we're a couple. We want the place because —"

"It's going to be a nursery for a future baby," Amanda finished for him, "or an office for my workshop that I use to sell cutting boards inlaid with seashells online."

"Cutting boards inlaid with seashells?"

"Dramatic flair. My character was lacking substance. There's always someone like that on these house hunting shows."

Bryce glanced back at Venus and thought he saw her smile. "Fine," he said. "As long as you help me keep the conversation going. And I'm not calling you another name."

"I'll save Cordelia Visell for a more deserving audience, then," Amanda smirked, walking up the steps with Bryce. Bryce rang the buzzer and it was only a few moments before Tom answered.

"Had to come see the place again?" The landlord asked, grinning.

"Well," Amanda stepped forward, "he didn't take any pictures like I had asked and I need to make sure it's got everything we'll need."

"Ah," Tom chuckled. "You must be the wife. Room's up this way."

Walking up the staircase, Bryce glanced over his shoulder and nodded to his ghostly companion. Venus nodded and disappeared, heading straight through the nearest wall. There'd be time to worry about her later, but Bryce could see the investigation was starting to frustrate her. Three days was a long time for anyone, especially if they couldn't sleep or eat. Bryce felt bad for Venus, but there was only so much he could do without getting into handcuffs.

"So," Tom said, opening the door. "It's got two bedrooms, one bath, in-unit laundry and—"

"Wow!" Amanda exclaimed, walking into the living room. "This is bigger than my whole apartment! Here wait, I need to measure this."

"She gets excited," Bryce chuckled, blocking Amanda from the landlord. "A lot of those home decorating shows go to her head."

"We see that a lot. New places can be—" Tom checked his phone and furrowed his brow. "Excuse me a minute. I need to take this."

Bryce waited until the landlord was out in the hall on the phone and relaxed. Amanda was walking slowly across the living room, stepping with her heel against the toes of her opposite foot.

"This place is humongous!" Amanda smiled, measuring her steps across the room. "You're telling me people actually live in places like this?"

"Usually with more roommates than there are rooms," Bryce said. "Don't get too attached. I think we're going to need to stall the landlord some more. The longer we can stay the better, and I can't keep him talking for long."

"How long will Venus need?"

"We stayed long enough for her to go through the first floor and most of the second. That means she has two and a half floors to go, so…maybe an hour to be safe? But I doubt we can justify staying for more than half an hour."

"I do have one idea," Amanda said. "Just play along and try to keep up."

"Wait, what's the plan?" Bryce asked.

"Sorry about that," the landlord walked back into the room, sliding his phone away. "Another prospective renter asking about the building, nothing to worry about. Any other questions?"

"Well," Amanda stepped forward and took Bryce's hand, "we just love it. I mean, you were not lying about this view, sweetheart."

"Why lie?" Bryce grinned back. Amanda dropped his hand and turned her lips downward into a frown.

"Oh, you mean like that time you *didn't* lie about staying late at work?" Amanda asked, venomous.

Bryce stumbled, but he recovered as fast as he could. "This again? I told you that my boss has me stay late some nights."

"Then why do I keep seeing pictures of you and the guys down at the bar when you're supposed to be working? It's like you don't want to be around me anymore."

"It's called networking, hon."

"So," the landlord cleared his throat, "the room starts at—"

"'Networking'? Is that her name?"

"Why do you always have to pick this fight?"

"I'll leave you to—" Tom gestured vaguely at them both. "It sounds like you have to work some things out. I'll be down in the front office. We have another showing at two, just so you know."

"I always pick this fight because you come staggering in at any hour you please!" Amanda snapped, undeterred by Tom's discomfort. "And don't think I don't notice another woman's perfume you on. Was that supposed to be your boss's or did it belong to your coworker?"

"Amanda, relax," Bryce grinned. "He's gone."

"Aw," Amanda frowned, disappointed. "I was just building real momentum there."

"Good thing he left or you might have smacked me."

"Could we? A red mark on your face would really sell the whole package."

"I think he got the point," Bryce smirked. "What made you think of that?"

"Arguments always make people uncomfortable," Amanda said, measuring out the living room with her feet again. "That's we try so hard to avoid them. It's easier to leave when other people are yelling."

"Well, next time tell me before we get in an argument?"

"I like the idea of a next time," Amanda nodded and looked out the living room window. The building was on a hill, looming over the city and providing a view beyond the brick wall of a neighboring building. Amanda folded her arms and sighed. "I thought working with a medium would be more exciting."

"Sadly," Bryce said, "exciting jobs like this don't come up often. Most of it is lying for the benefit of others."

"What's the worst lie you ever had to tell?"

"Not my lies."

"But for the sake fo the argument? I imagine it's not illegal for you to discuss past clients if they're...passed."

Bryce joined her by the window and looked out onto the cityscape. "Forgiving people is hard. Sometimes ghosts want a loved one to know they're forgiven for something. It's harder when I can tell they clearly don't mean it."

"That's a good lie."

"What about you?" Bryce said. "Any dirty lies you've told for someone else."

"Told my sister we had to take the dog to a farm upstate," Amanda shrugged. "Classic lie, but she was six, and we didn't want to tell her we had to put him down cause we couldn't afford the surgery."

"Yeah, the truth is harder for kids."

"Did you ever have to talk to a young kid for a ghost?"

Bryce stared out the window for a minute, focusing on the traffic passing by in the street just below them. "A mother wanted me to talk to her son for her. We found him playing in a park, but she got scared. I turned around and she was gone. Either she passed on after seeing him or it became too real and she ran off."

"Did you ever find her?"

"I don't go looking for ghosts. They usually find me. I like to imagine she got what she needed."

"That sucks she didn't get to say anything. I would have hoped she could say goodbye, at least."

"That's why I want to help Venus. Finding rest is important to every ghost. I think she deserves it more than anyone."

Amanda nodded and rubbed at her face, maybe to wipe away tears. She walked around idly, exploring the bedrooms and the bathroom. Bryce found her in the furthest bedroom looking out onto a highly obscured view of the lake in the middle of the city. "Truthfully, this is actually a nice place."

"If only there wasn't a murderer next door."

Venus was focused. Passing through walls was a question of mind over matter and she wasn't even thinking about the walls. She took in the contents of each room, getting a feeling of each person who lived there: baby's room, broke student, gamer, anime fan, someone really into their cat. Still, no one struck her as a killer.

Nearly passing into Frank's room again, the cold twist in Venus's gut made her stop before she could pass through the wall. Sacrificing precious time, Venus stepped out into the hallway and walked around the room, never turning her back on the feeling like it was a wild animal. It scared her more than the chance of finding her body. Once around the room, Venus completed her sweep of the second floor. Nothing struck her as strange, so she went up stairs to continue her search. She would have liked to take the elevator, but had no way to call it up without Bryce.

The third floor didn't have any killers, though Venus did quietly pass through the apartment where Amanda and Bryce were talking. They looked cute together and Venus didn't want to interrupt when Bryce didn't stop her. Despite the strangeness of their meeting, Venus could tell that Amanda was trying to get closer to Bryce and break down his barriers. It wasn't a bad match, in Venus's opinion. Bryce was a bit of a downer, but Amanda's usually happy energy seemed to balance him out. There were worse ways to meet someone these days.

Venus bounded up the stairs from the third floor to the fourth. These rooms were also empty of anything sinister besides the a quart of milk someone had left out on the counter that was starting to turn. A cat stared at Venus as she walked out into the hall after checking the final room. The rest of the complex was harmless, devoid of even the strong, sickening feeling that she got after walking near Frank's room.

"Guess there was only ever the hope, huh?" Venus asked, turning to the cat. The bright green eyes stared at her intently. Venus let out a breath and paced a little. She'd gone as far as she could go without finding anything. Still, it felt like Venus was missing something.

"The basement," Venus mused. "No attic, but a basement could hold something. Better than nothing, right, kitty?"

The cat hopped from its perch and rushed away, finally acknowledging Venus beyond the thousand yard stare. Venus hadn't seen a door down the basement and she didn't have time to hunt around for one.

"Floors are just walls, I guess," Venus thought aloud and took a deep breath. "And if I just focus that they're not there—"

Venus dropped through floors of the building, finally landing on hard cement. Even if she knew how to float, Venus doubted she'd have time to catch herself before the blunt impact of the concrete floor. Staggering to her feet, Venus rubbed her sore tailbone and looked around.

The basement was dark and cold, strictly utilitarian compared to the more aesthetically pleasing residential parts of the building. Venus walked around a little, unsure of what she was looking for. Most of the basement was taken up by the furnace and all the electrical wiring that ran up into the building. Everything was grimy and musty, dust covering the flatter surface. There was a storage shelf with basic handyman's tools and boxes marked 'Christmas Lights' or 'Halloween Decorations' on the side. None of the boxes were big enough to hold a body. At least, that's what Venus hoped. Venus found the stairs to the rest of the building, but her foot passed through the bottom step when her mind wasn't focused.

That feeling again. The intense, gut-wrenching sickness that made her head swim. She was too far from Frank's room. Venus took another step closer, passing through the staircase into the crawlspace.

The room was spinning, making Venus's stomach turn into knots. In the pitch black of the room, Venus couldn't tell if the negative energy of the room was choking her or if she had passed into a solid object by mistake. Slowing her breathing down, Venus focused on the room. Slowly, the floor came into focus, then the walls and window that was covered to only give a dim, ambient light. When her eyes adjusted to the light, Venus's stomach lurched.

There were piles of clothes down here: shirts, pants, shoes, and undergarments. The room spun and it took all of Venus's focus to see the room. She took a few steps towards the clothing pile, suffocating in the foul room. On top of the pile were a pair of blue jeans, a t-shirt, and beat-up sneakers. Venus's name tag was still attached to the white pharmacist coat.

Venus wanted to vomit. She felt the heaves coming, but she had nothing in her stomach. She had no stomach. Venus ran forcing her way to the staircase, struggling to breathe as she clawed her way up the stairs. She rushed through the door into the lobby. She was so focus on her escape, she barely registered going through the front door. Venus made it out the street and laid flat on her front, feeling the cool concrete against her flushed cheeks. She took deep, greedy breaths and pushed herself against the sidewalk.

The knowledge had left a hollow feeling in her chest. Venus thought that knowing would be enough, or at least make her feel better. All she could do now was cry on the sidewalk.

After about an hour of walking around the apartment, Bryce and Amanda finally agreed to leave. For appearances, Amanda stormed out the front door to wait for him. Bryce exchanged a joke about 'earning what was coming' before leaving the landlord for the day. He hoped they had bought Venus enough time.

"I think that was a lot of fun!" Amanda said, grinning. "I've always wanted to do something like that. I had an ex in college who took me on a date to test drive a ridiculously expensive sports car, but this was way better!"

"Cheap date," Bryce said, adjusting his coat.

"You brought me to a fake apartment showing, how is that not cheap?"

"We were not on a—Venus!"

Bryce rushed over to Venus, stretched out flat against the ground. Her body was trembling with heavy sobs. Bryce reached out to touch her, but his hand passed through her should. "Venus?" Bryce pleaded. "What's happening? This is not a good look for me."

"I—I—" Venus stammered out between sobs, "s-saw my name—name —"

"Your what? Your name tag? Did you find your name tag?"

Venus nodded and took a shuddering breath. "The basement..." she whimpered. "Down in the basement."

"The basement?" Bryce asked. He looked back to Amanda. "There's evidence she was here in the basement. We gotta call Clay. Come on, Venus, we gotta go."

Venus didn't move, unable to make eye contact with Bryce. Bryce looked anxiously up and down the sidewalk, looking towards the landlord's office window. He waved his hand in front of Venus's eyes, but she seemed to have retreated so far into herself that she wasn't seeing anything.

"What's wrong?" Amanda asked.

"She's...not good. I mean, we got the confirmation we needed, but—"

"It's a huge emotional blow," Amanda nodded. "Venus was always very sensitive. What can we do?"

"I don't know," Bryce shrugged. "I'm a messenger, not a therapist."

"You don't need to be a therapist, you just need to try. Has this never happened before?"

"I mean…once. I just left him."

"You left him?"

"Look, ghosts normally find their way back to me if we get separated. I've never had to help someone that I actually care about."

Amanda looked around and stood next to Bryce. "OK, this is gonna feel really stupid, but I'm in this deep. Point me at her. Where's her face?"

Bryce adjusted Amanda a little to her left so that the toes of her shoes were facing Venus's eyes. Amanda squatted down and looked down, pretending to tie her shoe. "Vee? Come on, we gotta go. You can't quit now. I know you're hurting and scared, but you never let me quit when I got scared. Remember what you told me about you in middle school? When you did gymnastics camp? You'd keep falling off the balance beam and you had all those bruises at the end of the summer? It doesn't matter how often you fall, as long as you—"

"—keep getting up," Venus finished with her. Bryce watched Venus take a slow, deep breath and put her palms against the sidewalk. She pushed and got to her knees before standing. She took another deep breath and looked over at Bryce.

"She's up," Bryce said, touching Amanda's shoulder. Amanda rose from her squat and brushed off her pant legs. Bryce and Amanda started walking, Bryce letting Venus walk ahead of them.

"I was right," Amanda muttered. "That did feel stupid."

"You did good," Bryce assured her. "And thank you. I don't have the best people skills. You spend your whole career talking to the dead and you kinda lose touch with the living parts of people."

"It shows," Amanda smirked, bumping his arm with her elbow. "By the way, you said you'd get me lunch for this."

"I'm a man of my word," Bryce smirked. "I can't promise anything special, but I got cash for burgers."

"Fine, but you're walking me back home. All this had me feel like I need more backup than my taser."

Bryce watched Venus, keeping her just ahead of them on the walk. Her gaze was fixed downward and her hands were deep in her pockets, but she stood a little straighter. Her skin had a bit more color back to it and she looked less tired. It was like a weight had been taken off her shoulders and she powered through using nothing but spite. Bryce had to admit that he admired that about her.

The group had gathered in Bryce's apartment, settling in the living room. Venus went to the couch and curled up on one end, huddling with her knees close to her chest. Amanda almost sat where she was, but moved closer to the center when Bryce instructed her.

"So," Amanda said, "we know where to send Clay. How do we get him there?"

"Venus said it was a secret room," Bryce said. "She only found it because she missed a stair."

"That's wild," Amanda said. "A room with no door and no idea who it belongs to?"

"Sounds about right. I don't know if there's any point in telling Clay if we don't know where to send him."

"Could we fake being like…city inspectors?"

"There's a difference between pretending to look at an apartment and impersonating city officials," Bryce said. "We need some way to confirm that there is a secret room *without* playing the 'ghost speaker' card. No court would believe that and Clay won't listen to me if that's all I got for him."

"OK," Amanda unfolded a napkin and uncapped a pen. "This is the building and here's the front door…"

Venus leaned forward and watched Amanda sketch the building. "That's wrong."

"What?" Bryce asked.

"What?" Amanda perked up.

"I was talking to Venus," Bryce indicated her spot on the couch. "What's wrong?"

"The basement doesn't match," Venus said. "The rest of the building is too long. The basement nearly lines up with the front door. The basement and foundation have to match."

"You said there was a window?" Bryce asked. "Somewhere light was coming from?"

"Here," Venus said, pointing to the far wall, "but it was covered with a piece of burlap or something."

"That might be something," Bryce said. "If we could get pictures from that window and show that the basement doesn't match the foundation—"

"Excuse me!" Amanda waved her arms to get Bryce's attention. "I can only hear half of this conversation."

"Venus is saying the basement ends more around here," Bryce said, drawing a line about three quarters through the sketch. "The other part is all the secret room. There's a window on the far side that Venus could see. We could look through the window, snap some photos—"

"Would that work?" Amanda asked.

"It's not proof of the secret room, but if we can get him in the right part of the apartment and look through the window? It's something. I'm gonna call Clay and see what he thinks."

Bryce stood up and walked into the bedroom, his phone already on his ear. Amanda looked down at the other end of the couch for a minute. She took the pen and wrote 'Yes' and 'No' on opposite sides of the napkin. When she was done, Amanda took off one of her big rings and balanced it the middle. "Alright. This is very stupid, but I'm doing it anyways. Yes or no questions. Make the ring fall the right way, got it?"

Venus walked to the other side of the coffee table and crouched down. She tried touching the ring a few times, but her finger passed through the metal band. Shaking out her fingers, Venus focused on pushing the ring over. She began chanting to herself. "Tip over, tip over, tip over—"

The ring toppled over and landed on the 'Yes' side of the napkin with a hard slap. Amanda jumped up and pushed further into the couch, catching her breath. Hesitantly, Amanda reset the ring. "Vee? Is that you?"

Venus smiled and pushed the ring over again. The landed on 'Yes' a second time and Venus pumped her fist into the air. Amanda took a few shuddering breaths and set the ring up again. "Is this a trick?

Venus pushed the ring over to the 'No' side of the page and cackled with glee. Amanda put her hand over her mouth and righted the ring.

"OK, um…shit! How are—no, sorry. Yes or no questions only. Is everything Bryce saying true?"

'Yes.'

"So, you're a…ghost?"

'Yes.'

"OK. Well, shit. And you didn't see a secret door?"

'No.'

"But there was a window?"

'Yes.'

"That's somewhere to start…"

"What are you doing?" Bryce grinned, walking back into the living room.

"I was talking to Venus," Amanda smiled. "What did Clay say?"

"I had to leave a message," Bryce looked down at the table and chuckled. "Homemade Ouija board? Good for when ghosts have trouble saying what they need. Pretty crafty…"

"I warned you she was clever," Venus beamed, pointing at Amanda.

"I just…" Amanda struggled for the words. "It's not that I don't believe you; I wanted more proof. Despite everything, I'm still not sure all the time."

"It's a lot to take in," Bryce sat next to her. "I didn't know Venus was at the point of manipulating objects yet."

"The ring is barely balanced," Venus smiled. "I just had to focus."

"That's the happiest I've seen her in days," Bryce told Amanda. "Moving a ring is a parlor trick. How about we move to my ouija board and see how talented Venus really is."

"Only if you promise not to cheat," Amanda said.

"I would never!" Bryce laughed pulling a chair up to his desk for Amanda. "That's a conflict of interest!"

Fifteen. Bryce counted fifteen seconds between each time the smoke detector's green light blinked. If he focused, he could just match his breathing to the light.

"Can't sleep?" Venus asked, more of an affirmation than concern.

"Nope," Bryce said, annoyed. "We're too close."

Venus turned back to the TV, an old sitcom rerun. Amanda was asleep in the bedroom, afraid to go home and too tired to resist Bryce's offer of his bed. Bryce took the couch, but knew wouldn't have slept any better in his bed.

Bryce had gotten used to waiting on Clay to cut through the red tape, but this felt different. When he was dealing with most ghosts, it was transaction. Talking about playing cards or bitter half-forgivenesses meant so little compared to this. Bryce had helped other murder victims in the past, but they always wanted to make the other person pay. Venus just wanted to rest and every minute they were waiting was another minute she wasn't at rest. Venus could be resting. Her killer could be in jail. Another body could be kept out of that basement.

"Screw it," Bryce said. He sat up on the couch and pulled his shoes on.

"What are you doing?"

"Clay wants evidence?" Bryce whispered. "I'll give him evidence."

"Bryce, you don't have."

"You saw piles of clothing down there," Bryce said, stern. "Whoever did this? They've been getting away with it with more than just you. I'm not gonna let this go on any longer."

"Then I'm coming with you," Venus said. "You'll need a lookout, at least. Maybe I can help you find the door into the secret room."

"Last time you were in that room—"

"I wasn't ready," Venus said, indignant. "I'll be ready this time."

Bryce tied his shoes and grabbed his jacket. He peered into his room to check on Amanda. She was deep asleep, pressing her face against a pillow she hugged. Bryce shook his head and closed the door.

"Not going to tell her?" Venus asked.

"I'm less likely to get caught if I go alone. I'm only bringing you because I'm the only one who can see you. I'll be back before she wakes up. Hell, I'll get coffee started for her."

"Tea," Venus corrected. "She prefers tea…strong, black tea."

"Thanks," Bryce said, closing his door. "I'll remember that."

Bryce locked the door to his apartment and walked as quietly as he could through the hall. The building at this time of night was eerily quiet. Even the creak of the last stair seemed sleepy as Bryce stepped on it. Bryce was relieved that the bus was pulling around the corner as he exited his building. Outside was cold and bitter, though Bryce wondered if it was just his mood.

Venus was quiet, taking the window seat and watching the dark world pass by. Rain pattered on the window as Bryce kept his eyes forward. It was a stupid idea, but he'd given Clay a chance. Bryce had to get photographic evidence so Clay would get a warrant. Red tape be damned. There would be questions, but Bryce figured his involvement would be forgotten after Clay found the room.

The bus shuttered through the rain, loose droplets getting swatted aside as the windshield wipers went back and forth. Bryce got off a few blocks away from Willow Grove Apartments. He was willing to risk the brooding clouds if he could get a drop on whoever owned the room.

"I'll go and make sure the room is empty," Venus whispered. "Don't get any closer until I give you the all clear."

"Careful," Bryce raised a hand in front of her. "I won't be able to help you off the floor this time. Keep your head and focus on the things that are real. The floor, the walls, the window…anything you can use to anchor yourself to reality."

Venus nodded and walked off toward the building, walking through the concrete exterior. Bryce waited, kneeling behind a dumpster to keep hidden.

Bryce rarely had the chance to do anything one would consider heroic. This was a special exception to his rule of staying uninvolved, but when he found out about the pile of clothing from Venus something in his gut twinged. He hated the idea of waiting for Clay and the police to do something. He couldn't make an arrest, but he could still do this.

"No one's awake on the first floor and the basement is empty," Venus said, reappearing by Bryce's shoulder. "The room is empty, too. If there's ever a time, it's now."

Bryce stood up and crept towards the apartment building, careful to avoid the first floor windows. Pressing close against the wall, he followed Venus through the alley and followed her to one of the windows at his feet. Venus pointed at the ground window. Bryce stretched out flat on his stomach and put his phone against the glass. A thick layer of fabric hid the room from Bryce's camera.

"I can do it," Venus said, reading Bryces confused expression. "I can get in there and lift the curtain."

"Venus, this isn't knocking over a ring or pushing a piece of plastic around. You'd have to grab hold of something for at least a few seconds at a time and lift it up."

"I can do it," Venus repeated, firmer. "Let me try."

Bryce let out a breath and shook his head. "It's not gonna be easy to stay in there for long."

"Then take your pictures quick," Venus urged, getting to her feet. "The sooner we wrap up, the sooner I get to leave."

"Venus—" Bryce started but stopped himself. "Be careful. Come out as soon as I'm done."

"I will," Venus promised. She took a step forward, passing through the wall and dropping out of Bryce's sight. Bryce stayed pressed against the wet concrete and checked both ends of the alley. The last thing he needed was someone surprising him and asking questions when Venus would only have a minute or two at most with the curtain. Before he had the chance to doubt her, the curtain started to move.

It took every ounce of concentration Venus could manage. It was almost embarrassing how much she was sweating with the effort of lifting a curtain. All of her energy went into an action she had taken for granted for her whole life. Inch by inch, the gap widened until Venus could see the lens of Bryce's camera.

"Hold it there," Bryce said, his voice warped by the glass between them.

"Hurry!" Venus urged him. "I don't know how long I can hold this."

The room filled with light each time Bryce's flash went off. Pain and nausea erupted in Venus's body all at once, nearly losing her grip of the curtain. Each time the room was bathed in light, the memories of the room came back stronger and more terrible. It hurt to think this was the last place her body had ever been. No one deserved that.

"Venus, focus!" Bryce told her. Venus shook her head and turned her attention back to the cloth she was holding. She focused on the curtain, the floor, the walls. These were real, not the fear or the sinking in her gut. Bryce took more photos adjusting his angle to try and get better views. Venus's focus was broken when the stairs concealing the room creaked.

"Someone is coming," Venus said, dropping the corner of the curtain. Bryce's silhouette rolled out of the way and Venus paused. This could be her only chance to see where the hidden door was. It could be her best chance to see her killer.

Wood protested until a rectangular entryway lit the room, casting a tall figure in shadow. Venus held back the urge to vomit or cry when she recognized the face of Tom.

The landlord passed a hand over his brow, wiping away sweat with his palm with a slight grin. He regarded the pile of clothing for a minute and Venus watched him carry a covered shape over his shoulder. As he set it down on the ground, a hand dropped out from under the blanket, lifeless and cold.

Rage suddenly burned inside Venus. Mustering all her strength, Venus shoved the man as hard as she could. Her hands made contact and the landlord tumbled over the body, scrambling back to his feet and looking around the room. Venus swung again, her fist making contact with his jaw. Tom's head snapped to the side and he looked around, panicked.

"Who's there?" Tom yelled. "Show yourself!"

Venus delivered a blow right into the man's solar plexus, a target she wouldn't have gotten if she weren't invisible. Her opponent punched wildly, swinging his arm through Venus's intangible form. Venus struck again, her elbow planting deep in his stomach. Tom looked around, angry rather than scared.

"Show yourself, coward!" Tom yelled, looking around. With a last push of effort, Venus shoved the landlord so hard that he went back through the door.

"You murdered me..." Venus seethed, stepping through the entryway. "You murdered them all! How many did you kill? Eight? A dozen? A hundred? No more...this ends now!"

The landlord scrambled away, looking up at Venus or through her into the empty room. Panicked, the landlord rushed up the stairs, leaving the hidden door open. Venus followed the landlord up the steps, determined and no longer afraid. She passed through the door in time to see Tom slam the door to his office and locking it behind him. Venus shook her head with disgust. He couldn't hide from her.

Venus took two steps forward and halted. She could probably kill him. Being able to fight him without risk of being hit gave her an advantage. She could push him down the stairs or into traffic. Maybe she could drop a heavy box on his head. Venus wondered if she could pick up a knife if she was angry enough.

A twinge of guilt, however, made her stop. Killing him would make her feel better, but that wasn't justice. There were other girls who had been brought to that basement. There were bodies she didn't know about and they needed justice. Death was too quick and permanent for Tom. Venus turned and walked away as a cold shiver passed through her shoulders. She couldn't lose control if she wanted to keep herself.

Venus stepped down the hall and passed through the wall into the alleyway. She stood over Bryce and waited. He nearly jumped out of his skin when he saw her standing by him.

"You okay?"

"No," Venus said. "I saw him. It was the landlord, Tom."

"You're sure?"

"There's a body in there," Venus affirmed. "Right now." When Bryce said nothing, she strode through the wall and landed in the secret room again. She lifted the curtain away from the window pointed to the hand. If the energy in the room hurt her, she felt far too numb for it to do anything now. She saw Bryce's camera flash a few times and she dropped the curtain, passing back into the alley with a jump.

"That should be plenty," Bryce confirmed. "Let's go."

Venus dragged her feet as she followed Bryce away from the apartment complex. The bus was empty again, so Venus sat on the window side and watched the rain falling. "I shoved him…" Venus said, hollow. "I yelled and I think he heard me. I could have killed him if I wanted."

"I could hear something," Bryce said, under his breath, "but wasn't sure how it ended."

"I couldn't do it. He's still alive in his office."

"Hey," Bryce whispered, turning to Venus. "That took courage. I know a lot of ghosts who would love to bury their killers."

"That wouldn't have ended this. Did you send Clay the pictures?"

"He's got plenty to investigate. I'm more concerned about you. That wasn't an easy thing for you to do. Going into the last resting place of your body, seeing a fresh corpse…letting your killer live."

"I feel…better," Venus said. "Not doing it. It wouldn't have been right. Not when there are so many people he's killed. I had to let justice put him away forever."

"We got enough to put him away. Normally, this might get me a few months in prison for trespassing, but Clay is smart enough to keep these anonymous. You did a good thing."

"I definitely scared him, though," Venus grinned, looking back at Bryce. "That felt good."

"He earned that much for now. I'll tell Clay to check there for him in the morning with a pair of handcuffs."

Venus nodded. She liked the sound of that.

Bryce woke up to the harsh buzzing of his phone against the coffee table. Reaching out, he fell off the couch and hit the floor, waking up him up quicker than he would have liked. Unlocking his phone, Bryce put the phone to his ear once he saw the name on the display.

"Detective Clay…"

"You're a reckless idiot."

"I'm sure you're right, but could you be a bit more specific?"

"We got our warrant for the basement based on your pictures. The door was still open and the landlord was in his office. It looked pretty—"

"Messed up?"

"Yeah. Hard to swallow. The landlord was very agreeable. Nearly turned himself in when we knocked on his door. I think I owe you an apology."

"Jail the bastard," Bryce croaked. "Put him where he can't hurt anyone. Then we'll call it even."

"We're gonna try and ID the other body and search the clothing for clues. Your friend Venus already came up. Maybe we can wrap up a few other loose ends."

"The Missing Person Department isn't going to be happy with you."

"They hate you more than me. You have a bad way of making them look bad."

"Thanks, Clay," Bryce said. "You took a risk. I appreciate that."

"Don't think this means I like you," Clay said. "You still technically trespassed, even if you had a ghost do the trespassing for you."

"You starting to believe me, Clay?"

"Go back to sleep, dumb ass."

Bryce chuckled and closed his phone. To his right, Venus was curled on the chair, looking hopeful.

"That's it," Bryce said. "End of the day, you'll have a closed murder case. Tom's going to jail. Everything tied up in a neat bow, courtesy of Clay."

"Good," Venus said, exhaling. "What's that mean for me?"

"Not sure," Bryce said. "Never seen a ghost pass on. Some people say there's a light at the end of a tunnel or a voice they hear. Usually a ghost will just—"

Turning towards the chair, Bryce didn't see Venus sitting there anymore. With a slight smile, Bryce leaned his head back on the couch. Venus was gone. "Take care of yourself, Venus."

Bryce sat on the floor for another hour, his elbow cocked on his knee while refreshing his phone until the news of the arrest broke. Amanda staggered out of the bedroom, trying to control her mess of pink hair. She cracked a smile and cleared her throat. "Hey…"

"It's done," Bryce said."

"What is?"

"They arrested the killer," Bryce said. "Clay went in this morning and the landlord confessed. Venus is gone."

"She—she's gone?"

"Yeah. She passed on to the next life."

"Where?"

"That's above my pay grade."

Amanda sat on the floor next to Bryce and looked at the opposite wall. "How did they know it was him?"

"They got some anonymous pictures and a hot tip."

"You should have brought me."

"You were asleep. You'd already done more than enough. Besides, Venus helped instead."

"Well, damn," Amanda dropped her shoulders. "I didn't think she'd leave so fast."

"They usually do. One minute they're there and the next?" Bryce whistled low with a wave of his hand.

"So," Amanda shrugged, "now what?"

"We get breakfast. I don't know about you, but I could use some pancakes."

"That's it?" Amanda asked. "We solve a murder, put away a serial killer and then go get brunch?"

"Can you think of a better end to a story than pancakes?"

Amanda shrugged and slipped into her sneakers. Bryce stretched and checked his phone again. The official story wasn't out, but Clay texted him that the landlord was processed and forensics was looking into the clothing.

"Do you want to collect Venus's things?" Bryce asked Amanda. "Clay is starting to pick through it, but since it's a closed case, they won't need it for long."

"Not today," Amanda said, fluffing her hair a little. "That feels like… admitting she's gone. I don't want to spoil our victory."

"That's fair," Bryce said. "Come on, there's a diner around the corner I've been to before. Big sign that just says 'Diner' in neon. Who knows if the food is any good."

"If they have tea and pancakes? How bad could it be?"

Bryce followed Amanda out the door and down to the restaurant. They sat on opposite sides of a long booth after a quick wave from a waitress. They put in their orders and Amanda offered to pay for Bryce's meal. "You did a good thing. You deserve breakfast on someone else."

The waitress left and Bryce folded his arms. He looked out the window to his left and watched a pedestrian ride by on a red bike. Bryce looked back to Amanda and smirked. "You want a job?"

"What?" Amanda asked.

"Do you want a job?" Bryce asked. "I hate to admit it, but it was nice having a partner that wasn't dead. It was fun working a case with someone else."

"This is a real offer?" Amanda asked. "I want to be sure you're serious about this."

"I can't promise consistency, but it would be nice to have back up I can rely on."

"I'll consider your offer if you consider mine."

"You have the floor."

"My roommate is officially dead and I'm back to living on my own. While I'll be okay for the next few months, it would be easier to keep things as they are if I had a roommate."

"Are you asking to live together?"

"Let's be honest," Amanda shrugged, "there's chemistry here. It may be Pop Rocks and soda, but it's still chemistry. I don't know what it is, but you're a good guy. And it would be easier to accept your weird job offer if I weren't trying to make rent on my own."

Bryce nodded and linked his hands together. "It might not work out. You don't have anyone else you could live with?"

"We just caught a serial killer, I'm pretty suspicious of anyone at the moment. You seem alright, if not a little weird."

"We'd need a bigger place. I'm not sleeping on that couch forever and I need space to do my medium business."

"Makes sense," Amanda said. "Maybe that two-bedroom place we were pretending to look at? The prices are low since they arrested the previous landlord."

"I could swing half of that. Sure you'd be alright with living in a haunted apartment?"

"As long as you can talk with the ghosts? Sure! Is this a common occurrence? Meet a ghost, solve a murder…get breakfast afterwards?"

"Sometimes it's too late for breakfast," Bryce shrugged, "but then I'll treat myself to a steak. I should warn you that I'm not well-liked by the police…or most grieving mothers."

"I worry that's in your delivery," Amanda said. "To be honest with you? You know ghosts, but you don't get people. You need my help with that."

"So…partners?" Bryce raised his coffee mug.

"Partners," Amanda grinned, tapping her empty mug to his. "This doesn't mean we're dating. This just sounds more interesting than waitressing, so don't get any ideas."

"Wouldn't dream of it," Bryce smirked.

The Star Map

Arielle woke up each morning for her shift at the coffeeshop, greeted by the glowing constellations she'd arranged on the ceiling. Maybe not Earth constellations, but she was almost sure they were constellations from somewhere. Arielle's room had always been a strange collection of oddities: animal skulls, interesting rocks or sticks, and books with the corners missing from being dog-eared so many times. She used to photograph the world around her. However, the constellations from elsewhere were her strangest obsession, leaving her camera untouched in her closet for years.

Friends frustrated Arielle when they told her that the star patterns were random. They saw idle designs that didn't mean anything, but the constellations weren't static to her. She would come home from her job at the coffeeshop, drop her backpack by the door, lay on her bed, and stare up at the homemade constellations. Her boney hands were kept busy braiding and unbraiding her long, blonde hair, but her mind was only focused on her map on the ceiling. She had to purchase over three hundred packets of stars to make her night sky the way she wanted.

It started with a packet of small stars she had arranged on instinct. After that, it was an itch. Arielle needed more stars. More stars were arranged by instinct, but it was different from the first time. She wasn't just placing them where they looked pretty. Arielle would agonize over the exact placement of each plastic star, ensuring it was where it needed to be. It was her obsession.

Arielle would lie and tell her friends that she needed to do her laundry or call her parents in Portland. However, she was constantly focused on the ceiling. She needed to build that galaxy, the map in her head. Arielle would show pictures of the constellations to friends and family, desperate to find someone else who saw the patterns burned into her mind.

"I don't see it," Maggie said, looking at Arielle's phone during a lull in service. Maggie turned back to the pile of mugs she was washing in the sink with a disinterested shrug. "It looks like you just threw them up there."

"It's more than that," Arielle urged. "It's…it feels like a compulsion. I need to put them there. I can't explain it."

"Have you seen a doctor about it?"

"I can't afford a doctor right now," Arielle said. "Besides it's not like it's affecting my life that much."

"How much have you spent these stars?" Maggie asked.

"I don't know…maybe three hundred and fifty dollars?"

"Arielle!"

"What? It's not hurting anyone."

"Well, then you better get to work if you wanna keep your star habit. Could you go bus that table? I gotta check the muffins baking in the back."

Arielle sighed and walked over to the nearest table, covered with piles of napkins around a large ceramic coffee mug that had been drained. She wadded up a handful of napkins and dropped them into the mug, but she stopped when she saw the ink on some of the wadded napkins. She unfolded one and nearly dropped the coffee mug.

"Arielle?" Maggie called from the counter. "Earth to Arielle!"

"Who was sitting here?"

"What?"

"Who was sitting at this table?" Arielle pointed at the table again, urgent. "Do you remember?"

"One of the usuals, I think," Maggie said, raising her hands. "Rail-skinny black guy with a close shave on the sides of his head. Never remember his name, so I just bring him his orders 'cause it's usually slow."

"When he comes in again, can you point him out?"

"Why? Is he doing something creepy?"

"No creepier than me," Arielle said, showing the connect-the-dots style diagrams the stranger had left behind. When Maggie didn't react, Arielle opened her phone to one of her star maps and overlaid the matching doodle, showing that they matched up perfectly.

#

Arielle spent the next few days watching the door. In her small college town, the usual assortment of artsy and corporate faces shuffled in and out of the coffeeshop without much to distinguish them. Still, Arielle perked up each time the door opened as if she was expecting an old friend or a new enemy to walk into the shop. She had saved the constellations from the trash and taped them together how they connected on her constellation map.

After three days of waiting, Maggie poked Arielle on the shoulder and pointed to young man walking through the door. After placing his order with one of the other servers, he silently crossed to the counter, grabbed a handful of napkins, and sat at one of the open tables. After making his coffee, Arielle approached him with his order.

"Where did you see those?" Arielle asked.

The stranger looked up, surprised that Arielle had asked him anything. He put a hand protectively over his napkins and pulled them away. "Nowhere. I just like making the patterns."

"Sure, but where do you get the patterns?" Arielle asked, leaning closer and dropping her voice. "Because you're not the only one who sees them…"

Arielle opened her phone, showing the constellations she had taken pictures of to catalogue her star map. Curious, the other man took her phone and adjusted the view on the screen. Recognition passed over his face and his eyes went wide with shock. He zoomed in and rotated one of the more detailed sections to get a better view.

Frantically, he reached into his backpack and took out a small, spiral notebook, flipping through the pages. He turned the notebook around and showed Arielle the patterns that matched one of her pictures. The star points had all been connected into a set of three progressively smaller circles, smooth despite the rough geometry of the other artist's art style.

"Everyone has their own name for it, but I call this one the Rings of Ryan."

Arielle took the page and held it next to her phone, surprised by the identical designs. "I call it Valkary's Breach."

"I'm Ryan."

"Arielle."

"Where do you see them?" Ryan asked. "In dreams or—?"

"No, not quite like that. I just…sense it? Where are these constellations?"

"I don't know," Ryan shook his head and sighed. "I've been drawing them for years."

"How many?" Arielle asked.

"Four years. You?"

"Four. Do you remember the exact date?"

"On three. One, two, three!"

"April 13th," Arielle and Ryan recited together. Arielle tensed and looked at Ryan oddly.

"What is happening to us?"

"Do you know about the Conclave?"

"The what?"

"OK, so you haven't been digging too deep," Ryan nodded. "There are a few other star mappers I've spoken to. Most of the ones I know are around the state, but there are a few others like us here in the city."

"How'd you find them?"

"Same way you found me. I asked the right questions, talked to the right people…sometimes I just got lucky. The point is that other people are making their own constellations using pen and paper, clay, wire and beads… I know one guy who uses toothpicks and marshmallows. Collectively, we call ourselves the Conclave of Constellations."

"Sounds like a cult…"

"We're not a cult."

"That's exactly what a cult says," Arielle shook her head. "So, what does the Conclave do?"

"Compare maps and try to figure out how everything connects. Everyone only seems to have a part of the map, but my constellations might fill a gap between two people's constellations and joins them. Your constellations might fight into someone's map."

"Do you all meet?"

"Online, mostly, but there's a few locals who get together, if you're interested."

"Why do we do it?"

"Meet?" Ryan asked.

"No, make the constellations."

"It's like…an itch. Does it need a reason? If you do certain drugs, your body craves it because of the chemicals it creates. It becomes the only way you can function after a while."

"But this isn't a drug or alcohol," Arielle urged. "These just started appearing in my brain one day and I can't stop creating them. How did they get there in the first place?"

"Some people think aliens," Ryan said.

"Some people are idiots."

"True, but what's your suggestion?"

Arielle had no snarky reply prepared for that. Ryan seemed genuinely interested, but Arielle wasn't sure if he wanted to help her or his Conclave more. Still, the urge to draw her star map made her want to know more. She thought it was something that she needed to complete. Working with others might be enough to give her her old life back.

"Where do you meet?" Arielle asked. "Someone's basement?"

"No, then we'd definitely be a cult," Ryan smirked. "We got a room at the library. We take our constellations, compare patterns and put them online to be processed into the Master Map."

"So, my stars might be part of someone else's constellations?"

"If you're lucky. We all get fragments and pieces of the larger whole."

"Mine is all one piece though," Arielle said, showing Ryan her complete star map. "It takes up my entire ceiling."

"Really?" Ryan looked over the whole map. "That's...odd."

"Why?"

"Most of us are lucky if we get full constellations," Ryan said. "Part of the reason we all look at each other's pieces is to try and find missing parts. When you connect with someone's pattern—when you see a full constellation? It just..." Ryan snapped his fingers and grinned.

"Do other people get big swaths of the map like this?"

"On occasion," Ryan said. "Some people will get a handful of constellations together, but it looks like you've been at this for a while. Maybe it's because you've been so focused on your map rather than looking at fragments other people have made. Charles—one of the local mappers?— he thinks that the star map was a message sent by aliens, but we don't have the technology to receive it, so a bunch of us just got fragmented sections."

"What do you think?" Arielle asked.

"I think he's got more ideas than I do and he's not asking me to pay for it. Look, if you have reservations about meeting the group? Let me help you set up your map in the database. They have algorithms running there all the time and it matches you up without having to put in extra effort."

"I guess I could do that. But somewhere public…I don't want to go anywhere alone with someone I just met."

"Library," Ryan pointed across the street. "I'll wait here until the shop closes today."

After her shift, Arielle was surprised how excited she was to put her portion of the star map up on the database. Ryan wasn't kidding. People from all over the country were looking to connect their fragments to other people. There were forums about everything from who sent the map to what people used to make their constellations. Arielle spent most of her time focused on building her constellations in the database.

Ryan helped her managed the controls at first, but Arielle needed little help arranging her stars after the brief introduction. She knew these stars and exactly where they went, no matter the medium she was working with. Ryan settled in with his notebook and started doodling more constellations while Arielle spiraled further into the database. By the time Arielle was finished, the library was preparing to close.

"You should check tomorrow and see if anything connects to your stars," Ryan suggested, lingering by the front door with Arielle. "Like I said, the algorithm goes all the time. It should be processed by morning."

"Thanks," Arielle said. "It was nice to talk about this without someone assuming I lost my mind."

"If you're mad, I'm mad. There are worse things to be. I'll swing by the coffee shop tomorrow, but we should do this again sometime."

"I'd like that," Arielle said. "I enjoyed that more than I thought I would. Until tomorrow? I have a very early morning to plan for."

Ryan waved good night and Arielle was able to go home and sleep without obsessing over her stars.

Arielle's alarm didn't wake her up. Her phone did. She was getting notifications so fast that her phone was vibrating non-stop. Annoyed, Arielle leaned over and checked what all the notifications were from. She had over three hundred emails from the Conclave Site. Each one meant her map connected to someone's constellations. Ryan texted her to break up the string of notifications.

<<Are you awake?>>

<<I am now.>> Arielle texted back. <<Why?>>

Before she could rub the sleep out of her eyes, Ryan was calling her. With a groan, Arielle unlocked the screen.

"It is two thirty in the morning and I work at five. This can wait until after my shift."

"Your map is blowing up!" Ryan urged. "The algorithm finished processing it about twenty minutes ago. I connected to eight of your stars myself."

"So, you're only eight of those emails that are keeping me awake?"

"Arielle, most people are lucky if their map connects to one other piece someone's constellations. You've connected to more people with one map than I've connected with in the entire time I've been on the site."

"So?"

"So, you've made a major breakthrough! We're connecting map fragments from all over the world, but that's not all, Someone figured it out about an hour ago. They think your map is the epicenter."

"The what now?"

"OK, remember the alien data packet theory?"

"That we couldn't decipher it because of our technology?"

"Right. Someone took your map and compared the fragments that connected with your map to local geography and it was like a splash zone. Whatever happened April 13th? It started here. And it looks like you got hit full on."

"That's a bold theory…"

"People are calling you the Star Prophet."

"Star Prophet?"

"It's one thing to have a big piece of the map, but one that binds everything together like this? It's like we only had the edges of a puzzle and you just solved a huge part of the middle. People are starting to wonder if *you* were supposed to get the message."

"What? Now I'm an alien on a conspiracy theory website?"

"No, but people are starting to notice you. Charles wants to meet at the meeting tomorrow."

"How does Charles know who I am?"

"I…may have bragged. Come on, it's not everyday I get to tell people I know a prophet."

"I'm not a prophet! I'm a barista at a coffeeshop, not Jesus!"

"Hey, Jesus was a carpenter first."

"Ryan, I swear to God…"

"One meeting in the library. Charles just wants to talk."

Arielle checked her clock and groaned. At this rate, she might get another hour of sleep at most. "Fine. When is your star mapper support group?"

#

After her shift, Arielle left the coffee shop and waited at the library for the rest of Ryan's group. Ryan came first at three and led Arielle to the study room on the second floor of the library. They'd barely gotten in when Ryan opened the door for a chubbier girl with wavy red hair and a pair of forearm crutches.

"Arielle, this is Maxine. Max, this is Arielle."

"The Star Prophet herself…" Maxine grinned.

"Just Arielle. I don't really feel comfortable with all the prophet stuff."

"Then call me Max. And I get it. It's a lot of responsibility to have thrown at you the first week with the Conclave. I work in lead pencil. How about you?"

"Glow in the dark stars."

"Clever!" Max grinned, dropping her shoulder bag on the table. "Probably helped you connect the dots faster than most of us…literally. I thought it was morse code at first."

The next person to come into the room had slim features and a thin build. Their hair was buzzed short and they had tiny metal rings lining the curves of both ears.

"This is V," Ryan said, pointing at the newcomer.

"Just the letter?"

"Easy to remember," V explained in a whisper like tiny bells.

"What's your medium?" Arielle asked, trying to pick up on the slang the others were already fluent in.

"Nuts and wire," V said, emptying the contents of their backpack onto the table and sending metal pieces clattering on the table. Dozens of nuts were all tied together with small pieces of wire that Arielle recognized as familiar constellations as V spread them out on the wood surface. "I maintain that three dimensions are better than two."

"Yeah, but maps aren't three dimensions," Max said, as if they had this argument a dozen times. "Unless it was a globe, but I don't think that's very likely."

"I think," Ryan said, smoothing the air, "V's point is that if we don't have the proper technology to receive the map, we shouldn't assume the same representations of space. Their maps could operate in four dimensions, for all we know. Hey, that looks like we have a match…"

"Where?" V asked, turning their pieces on the table.

"Arielle, help me out here," Max pleaded. "It's supposed to be flat, right?"

"I'm still pretty new to all this," Arielle raised her hands. "I just found out I wasn't the only one seeing things. I'd hardly say I'm the expert on this."

"Others would disagree."

Arielle perked up as another man entered the room. He had a balding head with hair along the sides of his head like grey clouds. He wore rectangular glasses and a square beard and mustache kept tight around his lips. His face was a little slack with age, but Arielle noticed the kindness in his eyes. With a wry smile, he extended a thin hand to Arielle. "I'm Charles. You must be the new kid."

"Ryan convinced me to join."

"Think of it like group therapy," Charles smiled, sliding out his laptop. "Talking about it helps you feel less alone."

"No offense, but you're not what as I was expecting when Ryan was talking about Charles…"

"Given the present company?" Charles said, powering on his laptop. "Seventy-eight years old. I was an astrophysicist turned science teacher before I retired. Then, when I started seeing the star, I knew they weren't our constellations right away. So, asking around, I found others who turned out to be in the Conclave."

"Most people are pretty remote compared to others," Max said, idly sketching in her pad without looking at the page. "Most places only have one or two mappers within driving distance of each other, but we're all in the same town."

"Lends more credit to the data packet dispersal theory," V said, fixing one of their constellation structures to the millimeter. "If our town — I mean, Arielle — was a focal point for whatever reason, we would be closer to the metaphorical blast radius."

"Which brings us to the first item on today's agenda," Charles said, rubbing his right eye with his index finger. "What does it mean?"

"I don't know," Ryan said. "But Arielle got more connections than anyone else on the Conclave site. This was a major piece of the puzzle, but we don't know what makes her so special. Beyond geography, what sets Arielle apart from other star mappers?"

"If we're going with pseudoscience?" Max asked. "There's the possibility that Arielle's brain is more receptive to their method of communication."

"Telepathy?" Ryan smirked. "That doesn't seem more plausible."

"We map constellations from beyond our solar system," Max shrugged. "I hardly think I'm an expert on plausible, but I'm keeping an open mind. Besides, you three said it was aliens. How is my theory less credible?"

"Maybe it's Arielle's actual brain chemistry?" V shrugged. "Visual artists tend to have the best luck as opposed to technically minded people. What if Arielle is just more creatively inclined?"

"I do some photography," Arielle shrugged. "But besides my stars, I haven't done any painting in years. Is there anyone more experienced in the Conclave that might have some answers?"

"Nothing concrete from our top brass," Charles said. "Lots of theories and plenty of arguing, but no one can agree on anything. A few people think our newest member might be able to navigate the map if we finish it."

"But where does the map lead?" Arielle said. "We keep calling it a map, not a chart. Maps are supposed to lead to something, so are we looking for like…a space pirate's treasure?"

"Wouldn't that be something?" Max lit up with a bright smile. "Blackhole Beard!"

"Allowing for some flexibility in the who and why?" Charles said, leaning forward like someone might overhear him. "The most common theory is that it's a calling card. Someone or something trying to meet with new species. Similar to how we sent out a satellite with information for other lifeforms."

"Yeah," Arielle said, "but Voyager was more than just a map with no understandable endpoint. We had music, piece of history, facts about or species…this is way less specific than that."

"Again, assuming we process information the same way as they do," Max said. "I'm a fan of inter-dimensional beings trying to get us somewhere safer to avoid catastrophe."

"And yet 'aliens' is a step too far?" Ryan asked.

"And if they're inter-dimensional, shouldn't they also think beyond two dimensions?" V asked.

"The point is," Charles said, raising his voice a little to refocus the group, "we have found someone who is incredibly gifted in something that we've barely begun to understand. Arielle might be able to complete the map."

"Could I see the map so far?" Arielle asked. "I haven't checked the Conclave site since I first uploaded the other day."

Charles turned his computer around and Arielle looked at the map of constellations. Her portion of the map was clear to her, a large portion of the upper right corner that she'd spent most of yesterday inputting into the site. Other portions of the map were filled in, like the edges of a jigsaw puzzle before filling in the middle. A few constellations floated in the middle of the blank space like they were trying to find where they connected, but none of the constellations matched Arielle's portion of the map in scope.

"It's far from finished," Charles said, indicating the abyss, "but we were all pretty excited when you filled up so much of the map at once."

"It still seems so empty."

"It is, but we hope you can fill in the rest."

"I'll try, but I make no promises."

"Don't doubt yourself," Max said. "You got farther than anyone else. Seeing the edges of the map can help me come up with inklings. Maybe it'll spark an inkling for you."

"Inkling?"

"It's a feeling," V explained. "Like when someone whistles the first bit of 'Shave and a Haircut'? You hear the rest without them finishing. It's kind like that. Only you don't know where the song came from, or how you know, or what the song even is…"

"You see someone else's stars and you know where the next star goes," Ryan simplified. "It's like building a connect the dots. Inklings are fickle, but they make more sense once you put them in your medium."

For the rest of the meeting, the others compared constellations and made notes. Without her preferred medium at hand, Arielle spent most of her time studying Charles's computer screen and watching the star map slowly expand, piece by piece. The librarian came by a few times, indicating their ever-dwindling time until the library closed.

"Same time Thursday?" Max asked as she tucked away her notebook. "I have that IT Certification class tomorrow."

"I'm game," Ryan said. "Arielle? Did we scare you off?"

"My shift at the coffee house ends at five. I can meet you all here."

Ryan nodded with a smile and helped V pick up their assorted constellations. Arielle held the door open for Max. "Hey," Max smiled at her. "I hope this isn't freaking you out."

"Honestly? It's nice not to feel so lonely about this stuff."

"Welcome to the Conclave," Max smiled, holding the elevator door open with a crutch.

When she got home, Arielle dropped her backpack on the bedroom floor and fell back on her bed, looking up at the spiraling glowing stars overhead. She rolled onto her side and took a few packets of stars from a box under her bed. Opening one, Arielle held up a star and followed the inkling forming at the base of her skull. By midnight, Arielle had covered half of the wall next to her bed and fallen asleep face first in a pile of plastic stars.

#

Arielle had Wednesday off. Usually, she took the day to clean her apartment, buy groceries and arrange her stars. Today, Arielle converted her new constellations to the Conclave site before running her errands.

<<I see you've been busy.>>

<<Inkling came when I got home.>> Arielle texted back. <<I spent most of the night doing it.>>

<<Well, everyone is praising the prophet's return. Congrats, you're a legend.>>

<<Has the algorithm finished already? I turned my email notifications off so I could sleep.>>

<<Let's just say you should check.>>

Opening her email, Arielle nearly dropped her phone at the seven hundred and fifty-six emails from the Conclave site.

<<How are there so many more?>>

<<Some are people building off yours from two days ago. A lot more are from the top portion of the map you filled. Max was texting me all morning, you connected like…9 of her constellations. V got pinged for 4.>>

<<You?>>

<<5.>>

<<This is bonkers!>>

<<Need to let off steam? I can get you a free lunch at the burger joint on Fifth and Main.>>

<<How?>>

<<I work the counter. Swing by at two. It'll be slow enough that we can talk.>>

After she'd brought her groceries home, Arielle went to Fifth Street Burgers and hopped on an open stool at the counter. Ryan took her order and chatted quietly with her between customers. When Arielle's lunch arrived, she took the top bun off her burger, grabbed a handful of potato chips, and stuffed them on top of the rest of her sandwich dressings.

"That's weird," Ryan laughed, wiping down the counter with a towel.

"Say what you like, but I prefer a little crunch," Arielle said and licked grease from her fingers. Her phone buzzed again and she angrily shoved it into her backpack.

"Still going strong?"

"I'm almost up to a thousand emails today. I'm gonna have to upgrade my inbox storage at this rate."

"How does it feel?" Ryan asked. "When I get a constellation connected, it feels like I accomplished something. It's a relief to have it mean something. What's it like to get all those constellations to connect?"

"I don't really feel anything. Most of the time I struggle like anyone does with constellations, but last night was different. One minute, I'm staring at the ceiling and putting stars where they felt right. The next, I'm waking up, peeling stars off my face and realizing the full scope of what I've done. And it's still so clear in my brain. It's…pure creation. No thinking, just visualize and create, visualize and create. I don't even hesitate after I found my stride."

"Sounds great. It must really take the edge off."

"I've been able to focus all day," Arielle nodded. "Since joining the Conclave, I feel like a normal person again."

"Well, even prophets can stop for a burger now and then."

"Can I ask you something?"

"Sure."

"Do you ever want to quit? Like, have you ever packed away your notebooks and gone where you can't think about it?"

"First year it started happening, I quit at least once a month. Last time I did it, I drank pretty heavily one night, woke up hungover, and—while curled up by the toilet—sketched out eight constellations on my bathroom floor with a magic marker I'd stolen the night before. You thinking about hanging up your stars?"

"Wondering if I ever could. I went to my sister's for a week last August, but I ended up coming back with a dozen new constellations. I was almost upset with myself for taking so much time away."

"It's good when you finish, but it's a pain in the ass."

"Amen," Arielle raised her milkshake and took a sip. She talked occasionally with Ryan when he wasn't talking with other customers and noticed when he would doodle constellations on the backs of unused napkins when there was a lull in their talks. At the end of her meal, Arielle took a final slurp of her milkshake until the suction reverberated back through the top of the glass. Setting her clean plate aside, Arielle drummed her fingers on the counter and rubbed her eyes. "I think I'm gonna go take a nap. I was up too late last night to function. Thanks for lunch."

"Come around whenever you want. I get a free meal every shift, so I can hook you up."

"Thanks," Arielle said. She took out her wallet and dropped a few bills on the counter. "For tip."

"*That* you can always do," Ryan smirked, folding the money and putting it in his pocket. "See you tomorrow?"

"Yeah, for sure," Arielle said. She walked out into a bright and cloudless day, but constellations still danced in her head.

When she got home, Arielle pushed the thoughts of stars and space out of her mind. She fell back on the mattress and tried to close her eyes, but the constellations above her weren't finished. She tried rolling over, pressing her face firmly into the pillow, but the phantom specks that filled her eyes only formed new constellations.

In a moment of clarity, she knew that the star map would lead to something. It wasn't just a lesson from aliens or a puzzle from inter-dimensional beings. It wasn't a shared hallucination or some kind of government experiment like some people thought. There was a goal. As she was thinking about it, a word boomed in her mind until she said it aloud. "The Ark."

"Like…Noah's Ark?" Max asked. Arielle had explained her revelation to Max as soon as they were both in the study room. They were both a little early, but Arielle felt like she was going to explode if she didn't talk about it.

"I think so?" Arielle said. "I just got this feeling that it was the right word. It felt like an inkling, but it was word, not a pattern. I think it leads to the Ark."

"But how do we find it?"

"I looked up at the star map over my bed," Arielle said, pulling up the map on her laptop. "I feel like this is a map, but it's not an 'X' marks the spot. We use terms like inklings and itch when we're working on the map. What if finding the endpoint is just part of the data packet? That's why it's so hard to just stop. We need to see the finished map in order to know where the end is. I know that it sounds—"

"It doesn't though, that's the weird thing!" Max agreed. "It makes perfect sense. Like…I'm a famous rage quitter. When things are too hard for a situation, I always walk away. But I can't stop with this map. Maybe you're onto something. But where did the word Ark come from?"

"Same way I get impressions of constellations. It just popped into my head and nearly ached until I said it out loud."

"Maybe this is part of the invitation? Some higher beings—I still refuse to say aliens—built this Ark or whatever and if you're smart enough to get and understand the map, you can come contribute your culture to the Ark or something."

"Or it's a safe?" Arielle nodded. "A big genetic vault for whatever this being is. They're telling us how to find them and…and I don't know, help restart their species with our own genetics?"

"I hope that we don't have to be too involved in that process," Max scrunched her face. "Morally, I'm not super opposed, I just don't know how the biology would hold up."

"Best part of the conversation?" Ryan asked, setting his back down on the table. "Or worst part? Everything OK?"

"Arielle had a vision."

"It's not a vision," Arielle corrected. "Just a theory."

"She had an inkling—" Max continued.

"So?" Ryan asked, dropping his notebook on the table. "I get three inklings before breakfast."

"About where the star map leads? Ah! Thought that would get your attention."

"Seriously?" V asked, poking their head in, followed by Charles. "Where does it lead?"

"I don't know, but the word 'Ark' came to me last night while I was trying to fall asleep. It felt the same way a constellation does but it was a word."

"That's…very interesting," Charles said. "Start from the beginning…"

Arielle told her story again, feeling less like a raving lunatic. The others would ask questions and confirm details, but no one questioned the validity of her story or even the details. They all spent time trying to figure out what the Ark was, but without more details, they could only guess.

"Maybe the rest will come in time?" V shrugged their shoulders. "I know it's not a lot, but maybe there's some more information you can get?"

"Don't push yourself too far," Charles cautioned. "I've heard of people getting so deep into trying to figure out the map that they burn themselves out."

"This is big news," Ryan said. "Do we share it with the Conclave?"

"For now?" Charles scratched his beard. "I'd say no. I don't want to put too much pressure on Arielle by making this public. If she gets more inklings, that's good news. However, I'm hesitant to put her front and center on the forums. Arielle's mapping is good, no question. However, if she starts talking about visions, I doubt anything could keep people from turning this into a religious following. It's up to you, though, Arielle."

Arielle looked down at her hands, sore and tight from wringing her fingers together all afternoon. Announcing to her group had felt better, but she also wanted to tell as much of the Conclave as would listen to her. Still, Charles made a point. She had gotten an inkling about what was at the end of the road, but there was still too much unknown. She rationalized that she could always tell people later. It was harder to take something like this back.

By the time the others were wrapping up, Arielle had covered a whole page of Ryan's notebook paper with words related to 'ark', but nothing electrified her brain like the first inkling she'd gotten. The others had done some work, but only V was satisfied with the configuration of nuts and bolts that they were calling 'The Wrench of the Universe'. When the librarian knocked on the door, Arielle was ready to leave.

Max, Ryan and V left together to grab dinner, but Charles stopped Arielle before she left. "If you get anymore inklings," he whispered. "Let me know. Here's my number. I want to help you figure this out."

"Thanks, Charles," Arielle nodded. She took Charles's business card that still said 'physics professor' for his title and left with the others, eager to eat with them after pouring her thoughts out onto the page.

#

At home, the star map spiraled overhead. Arielle had moved all the furniture out of her bedroom, leaving the walls and ceiling completely open for more stars. Her mattress was in the middle of the floor and unpackaged dozens of packages of stars, scattering them on her blanket. She didn't have work until later today, but her mind was already spiraling into the stars overhead.

The word 'Ark' kept drifting in her mind and she wanted to complete the map, but she had no idea why. Even if she could finish the map, would it be enough to satisfy the itch? She couldn't get there, even if she knew where 'there' was. She picked up her phone and tapped at the screen while she formulated her message.

<<Why are we doing this?>> Arielle texted Ryan.

<<What do you mean?>>

<<What's the point of all this? It's not like we can ask for a loaner from NASA.>>

<<Until yesterday, I didn't even think there was somewhere to go.>>

<<I want to tell everyone. Maybe there's someone smarter than me who could figure it out.>>

<<Charles is probably right, but if you think it's important? I'd tell people. The Conclave's strongest asset has always been the members.>>

Opening the Conclave site on her laptop, Arielle started a new forum topic recounting her inkling experience with the Ark and was asking for anyone to help her decipher the message. She didn't expect anything, but just putting it on the site felt better.

Arielle closed her laptop, squinted a little and turned her head, adjusting her view of the stars. The mapping was becoming difficult again. She did her best not to strain her eyes, but the itch to finish her map was overwhelming. The Ark was important. She had the information for a reason. Her phone buzzed again, but instead of a text from Ryan, it was a message on the Conclave forum about the Ark.

The forum was abuzz with rumors of a treasure at the end of the map and people were eager for a finished map. People were saying they were calling out of work to work on the map, handing their children off to spouses and grandparents, turning their lives upside for a chance at a final destination. Everyone was demanding more information from the Star Prophet.

Arielle dropped the phone on her mattress, kicking it away as if it were a venomous creature that bared its fangs. She huddled close, holding her knees tight against her chest and looking around her room at the expanding star map. It felt like she was floating in space, suffocating in the lack of air. The stars around her seem to glitter.

Respond

The word made Arielle gasp and she took a deep breath of air. She coughed and rolled off her bed, desperately panting on the floor. When the inkling came, it was like the word had been stuck in her lungs before she could say it. However, this time the revelation rang in her mind in a voice that wasn't her own.

#

"My insurance won't cover an MRI," Arielle said, rubbing her face. "I'm not even sure what would come up."

"Arielle," Maggie pleaded, "why are you doing this to yourself? All this…star nonsense is driving you out of your mind!"

"I'd be worse if I weren't talking to the people who actually get it!" Arielle snapped, making a few customers look up for their laptops and glare. Ignoring the stares, she turned around and furiously scrubbed a coffee cup in the sink.

"Arielle," Maggie said, a little calmer, "what happens when you get a panic attack — or whatever this is — while you're on your shift? What if the boss catches you doodling stars on the backs of napkins and unused coffee filters? And now you're talking about hearing voices? Do you hear yourself?"

"I'm not the only one," Arielle said. "You don't understand. I've been stumbling through this for years and now that I've met others who understand it? It's such a relief to know I'm not broken."

"You can have two broken cups," Maggie said, "but they're both still broken."

Maggie was about to say more, but the bell at the counter rang. Ryan gave Arielle a small grin and a quick wave. Pushing passed Maggie, Arielle went up to the counter and forced a smile.

"Everything okay?"

"Besides the auditory hallucinations, panic attacks and lack of sleep? Peachy. What's up?"

"I just need some coffee. Black…whatever's in the pot."

"Got it." Arielle punched a few buttons on the register and grabbed an empty mug. Ryan passed over a twenty.

"Keep the change. I know this hasn't been easy."

"Any word?"

"'Respond' seems to be a pretty clear statement. The good news is, we don't need to crowdfund a rocket ship to get our lives back."

"We just have to figure out how to transmit a message that we don't know what to say with technology that we aren't sure exists."

"We'll figure something out. Tell you what, tonight is V's birthday. Why don't you come? Let off a bit of steam and get your mind off things. I know they'd love to have you come."

"You think?"

"We've gotten kinda fond of you. Besides, V's working on something you're going to want to see."

#

V's apartment was the basement level of a house about twenty minutes from the coffee shop. The apartment had a simple kitchen, a bed, and a computer with a large monitor on the wall. The screen was filled with a constantly updating star map with a smaller portion of the screen constantly shifting constellations until it determined the appropriate place for one or passed. Around V's bed were three large tubs filled with different sized nuts and washers. A large coil of wire and V's pliers were on their bed, evidence that they'd been working before Ryan and Arielle arrived.

"Nice place, V," Arielle said, walking over to the large monitor. "Is this the Conclave site?"

"Algorithm 2.0, I hope. It not only looks at constellations how they've been entered, but also rotates and inverts them. It builds off of my three dimensional theory."

"Does Charles know about it?"

"I'm submitting the code to him next week. I've had the software processing all the individual pieces from the Conclave site for about two days and it's going much faster than the last formula."

"And it's accurate?" Arielle asked.

"As accurate as the Conclave site," V smiled. There was a sharp knock on the door and Ryan peered through the window before opening the door.

"I'm late, I know!" Max panted, closing the door behind her. She crossed into the kitchen and carefully removed her backpack. "However, I come with the gift of booze for the birthday person!"

"Then you are forgiven," V affirmed, reaching deep into the backpack. V pulled out a handful of beers and distributed them to the others.

"No Charles?" Max asked, sitting and setting her crutches under her chair.

"He had other plans, I guess," V shrugged. "He gave me a card, at least."

"Impressive that he has a social life at seventy-eight," Ryan said.

"More of a social life than of us, I'd say," Arielle laugh. "I think this is the first party I've been to in a year."

"Then a toast!" Ryan said. "To our newly twenty-one-year-old insomniac! Long may they reign!"

"Here, here!" Max cheered, taking a sip from her brown bottle. Arielle took a swig, but her eyes kept going back to the screen.

"We can cover it if you want," Ryan offered. "Could we turn it off, maybe?"

"No, it's fine," Arielle rubbed her eyes. She was starting to see spots again. "I just thought I saw something."

"Another inkling?" Max asked.

"Hey, come on," Arielle said. "Tonight's about V. Besides, I'm trying not to think about it. I need to be able to treat it like background noise."

"That's the only way I can do anything," V said, sitting on the bed while Arielle and Ryan pulled up chairs between the kitchen and the bedroom. "Too much quiet and my brain just fizzles out trying to sort through all the dots."

"I talked to this guy in Berlin?" Max said. "He actually hears the constellations as music."

"Really?" Ryan asked.

"Yeah, he showed me some sheet music. He's a concert pianist, so sometimes he'll just play quick tunes in his head and then he sketches out the notes and, after some adjustments, it comes out like a constellation. He has this one ditty called 'Orbits' and it's beautiful."

"That's wild!" V grinned. "I thought seeing things was weird, but hearing things is—oh, sorry, Arielle."

"It's alright," Arielle grinned. "It is pretty weird."

"What did it sound like?" Max asked, leaning forward. "The voice, I mean. Man? Woman? Neither?"

"Max…"

"I'm just curious, Ryan. Not only is she the best star mapper in the world—and don't say she's not—but she's getting messages none of us are getting from the sender. That's gotta mean something."

"I don't even know what this 'sender' wants," Arielle said. "All I've heard is 'Ark' and 'Respond' so far."

"It's interesting that it came to you in English," Ryan said. "Knowing there's no language barrier makes things easier."

"Since it seems that the constellations come to us through the creative center of our brains," V theorized, holding their untouched beer close to their lips, "it might also pass through the language center in a few rare cases, like Arielle."

"Right," Max nodded. "If we knew more about how the message was supposed to be received, maybe we'd have a better idea of what to do with it."

"I mean, what can you even say?" Arielle asked. "If you knew aliens or higher dimensional beings were listening?"

"How about 'Get Lost'?" Max laughed. "Seriously, I don't care if they turn me inside out or whatever. None of us signed up to deal with this."

"Agreed," Ryan said. "I might say it slightly friendlier to avoid any inversion, but I would be better off without these visions."

"I wouldn't," V said, still rolling the bottle in their hands. "I like them."

"Why?" Arielle asked. "Don't they ever bother you?"

"Sometimes. But I wouldn't have met you if I didn't get them."

There was a shared grin between the others and Ryan shook his head with a smirk. "Sap..."

"To friends made in adversity?" Arielle offered, raising her beer. "When we finally figure this out, let's stay friends."

"Agreed!" V raised their bottle and finally took a sip of their drink. Instantly, they spat the beer back out and coughed. "I waited twenty-one years for this?"

#

Arielle was in space. She could tell by the constellations around her that she was in the star map. Seeing the stars fully realized, Arielle was slightly in awe as she looked around the galaxy. Turning around, she saw three other human forms in her galaxy. Lit from behind, she couldn't make out their faces, the beings were facing off against like they were separate corners of a square. In the middle of the square was a small, spinning globe.

When Arielle took a step forward, the others followed her motion. She took a startled step back and the others mimicked her. Curious, Arielle noticed that the other three did what she did and mirrored her movements. Slowly, the four beings converged on the globe, step by step.

The sphere was black and completely smooth. Even closer, Arielle couldn't see anything remarkable about it, but it felt significant. She wasn't sure if it was something she needed to learn about or remember, but there was something about that felt like an inkling in the back of her head.

"Unite."

This wasn't Arielle speaking. She didn't think it was any of the other beings judging by how they all sought out the source of the voice. They turned their heads from side to side, as alarmed by the strange voice as she was. Tentatively, Arielle reached out a hand and pressed her hand against the sphere. The others touched it in unison with her, the collective hands engulfing the globe. The orb was warm and thrummed with a chaotic pulse. Like a thousand heartbeats fighting to be heard beneath the surface of the globe.

"Unite," the voice repeated, firmer this time. Arielle moved her hand, sliding it up the globe until all four beings touched fingertips. The heartbeats pulsed clearer, unifying until Arielle could feel the steady thumping in her bones. For a moment, she could see the outlines of the other humanoid faces. Arielle squinted against the bright light behind her cohorts, but she could only make out the bright sunbursts of their eyes against the pitch black of their faces. Arielle was about to speak when she woke up in a cold sweat, gripping her blanket tightly to her chest.

Unfolding her stiff fingers from the blanket, Arielle took a deep breath and started relaxing her body. It was a difficult process to focus on each muscle, but eventually she felt like she wasn't readying for a sprint. Once she felt she had control of her body again, she grabbed her phone and typed out everything she could remember. The four beings, the globe, unity…it all had to mean something. She almost went to the Conclave website and started a new forum. Charle's warning, however, made her stop. After what happened with her revelation of 'The Ark,' Arielle needed to be more cautious about what she posted on the forums.

Arielle needed to talk to her friends. Her logical brain assured her it was nothing—too little sleep, too much mapping, too much stress—but a twist in her gut made her second guess that judgment. She set her phone aside and sank back into her mattress. Her body ached liked she'd run a marathon. Her anxiety eased only slightly once she was able to put her scattered thoughts in order. The image of the globe and the idea of 'unite' still hung over her like a cloud, threatening to smother her with the sudden realization of their meaning.

#

"So, these others," Ryan said. The study room was silent when Arielle had told everyone about her dreams. "None of the others had faces."

"They were just…shapes," Arielle said. "I could only make out the eyes because they were brighter than the rest of the face. It was like a fun house mirror, but when we touched fingers I felt—"

"Electric?" Max asked, chewing the eraser of her pencil.

"Not really. It was like…for a minute, I felt like the world was vibrating. And then all the chaos reduced to a single pulse and—"

"Like a heartbeat?" Charles asked.

"I thought that might have been it at first, but now I think it was something else."

"If you heard it or felt it again, would you recognize it?" V asked.

"What do you mean?" Ryan asked.

"So, obviously we've been trying to figure out how to communicate with these senders," V said. "What if they communicate through these pulses and wavelengths?"

"Are you suggesting some Close Encounters of the Third Kind sort of thing?" Ryan asked.

"Why not?" Charles shrugged. "If this is some kind of alien race that can still communicate with us, there has to be some way of communicating back. Most of our Earthling communication technology relies on translating pulses and wavelengths, after all."

"Exactly," V smiled. "I think, if we can figure out what their frequency is, we can mimic it, at the very least. Let them know we received and understand their message."

"How? We don't speak any of their language." Ryan asked.

"We do, though," Arielle said. "I at least get it translated for me. If they sent it the same way they sent the star map, maybe I have more of their language hidden in my subconscious. The map did fall into my metaphorical lap…maybe I'm more attuned to it than others."

"And once we have our message," V said, excited. "Maybe we're supposed to transmit it to wherever the star map leads?"

"With what?" Ryan asked.

"I think, with some help," Charles said, "we could jerry-rig a basic transmitter. It wouldn't be very powerful, but we'd only really need to break the atmosphere. Maybe the map is meant to give us a clear shot at the senders…like an interstellar mailing address."

"The Ark," Arielle said. "We're supposed to contact the Ark."

"And then…they come visit?" Max asked. "Sorry, but I'm not a huge fan of 'Open Invitation to Earth: Invasions Welcome.'"

"It didn't feel that way," Arielle said. "It was…I don't know, the sender's voice has always been more curious than malicious. It felt more like an invitation for us."

"To do what, exactly?" Ryan asked.

"Say hello?" Arielle shrugged. "I don't know. We've been searching for alien life for as long as we've had a space program. I don't see a reason to ignore an invitation. Maybe it's a wolf in sheep's clothing, but what if it's legitimate first contact?"

"What if we put it to the Conclave?" Ryan asked. "Tell them our idea and have everyone vote on it? Maybe even contribute?"

"Elections, especially digital ones, can be hacked," V said, barely whispering the thought aloud.

"You think there are special interest groups who don't want us to make contact?" Ryan asked.

"I'm more concerned with the opposite."

"I'm with V," Arielle said. "Putting the decision out in the open is a risky gambit we can't take. We're already raising a lot of eyebrows with this Star Prophet stuff, I'm sure. I don't want to draw too much attention."

"Seconded," Charles said. "If we do this? We do it on our own terms."

"I'm sure their receiver technology is better than ours," V said. "I could probably whip something together to make a strong enough signal with enough time."

"Max?" Arielle said. "You're being quiet…"

"I just—what if this isn't an invitation? What if it's bait? I'm not saying I don't trust Arielle, but a smile is a mask that anyone can wear. We should be careful. Even if our new friends are waiting for a reply, something else might be lurking in deep space and waiting for our signal. What if like… Predator or something hijacks the signal and comes after Earth?"

"Well, the aliens from Predator already know where Earth is," Ryan said. "They keep coming back. That's the plot of the second movie."

"At any rate," Charles cleared his throat, refocusing the conversation. "We won't know anything until we have a full map. I think we can play with this idea, but we should put a majority of our efforts into completing the star map. The pulse idea is something, but it won't be any good if we can't figure out where to send anything. We need a completed map."

"Oh my God," Max's jaw dropped and her hands slowly slid away from her laptop. "It's gone…"

"What?" Arielle asked.

"The Conclave site…the map, the forums, everything is gone, it's totally blank!"

"What do you mean?" Ryan asked, panicked and looking at Max's laptop. "It can't be gone!"

Arielle took out her phone and opened the bookmark she had for the Conclave site. The screen reported that there was no site at the address she had entered. After she refreshed the page twice, she typed it in by hand and then tried disconnecting from the wifi to check if it was the network. Nothing changed.

"Is it a glitch?" Arielle asked, surprised by the fear in her voice. "Maybe they moved?"

"They would have told us," Charles said, frantically typing into his computer. "We moved once already, but they wouldn't have done it again without warning! I would have known!"

"It's gone…" V whispered, hopelessly scrolling the blank page on their table. "Everything we worked for is…gone."

Arielle felt like she was drowning in space again.

#

"Any word from Charles?" Max asked. She stabbed at her fries with a discarded toothpick while V checked her tablet again. Arielle had barely eaten any of her burger, despite Ryan's urging.

"Nope." V shook their head and put the table away. "I can't believe this. It feel like someone just…died."

"Yeah, it kind of did," Max said. "It took hundreds of people four years to fill in as much as we did. And we don't even have a way to communicate with most of them. We just went from an army of star mappers to a lonely platoon."

"Any news about another site starting?" Ryan asked, hovering by the table to refill a coffee cup. "I found the initial site by browsing online forums after a web search…"

"Even the social sites are squeaky clean," V said. "Facebook groups: gone. Reddit threads: gone. Twitter feeds—"

"Okay, okay! Christ, we get it." Max snarled.

"Max…" Arielle chided.

"I know, I just…it feels like we got cheated. We did all this work and collaborated from all over and now it's just—" Max struggled for the words, but eventually settled on blowing a raspberry. Arielle chuckled a little, but agreed with the sentiment.

"Maybe there's someone we can call?" Arielle asked. "Whoever is in charge of the website?"

"The only person we know of is Charles," Ryan shrugged. "He was one of the site founders."

"He was?" Arielle asked.

"Yeah," V said. "That's how we found out about the site in the first place. He found me working in the library."

"I was caught sketching on the bus," Ryan said. "I found Max at the restaurant. Then you found me in the coffeeshop."

"Has anyone…ever seen Charles map?" Arielle asked. There was an odd moment where it felt like no one wanted to answer, even if they knew.

"I think I saw…no," V slouched. "He was just sketching out one of mine."

"I thought he worked on his computer?" Max guessed. "Isn't that what he's always doing at the table?"

"I always thought he worked at home," Ryan said. "But he's never even shown me a constellation, now that I think about it. He's always had more of an…organizational role."

"He's from…Texas right?" Arielle asked. "Why is he up here?"

"He moved here just after—" V started, but the words suddenly became difficult. "—after we all started mapping."

"So, he just…got up and left a teaching job to travel here?" Arielle started looking between the others. "Did he suggest the 'Data Packet' theory?"

"Hold on, what are we accusing Charles of?" Ryan asked.

"At the moment?" Arielle started. "Nothing. I'm just wondering why he never comes out after our sessions. We invited to V's birthday. He didn't even want to come out tonight."

"Yeah, but…he said he was busy," V said. "Do you think…Charles had something to do with the site being taken down?"

"He said he would have known if the site was moved," Arielle said. "But he never said that he *didn't* know."

"He didn't want us to finish," Max growled. "Once we gave him enough information, he must have figured enough out."

"But why cut out the rest of the star mappers?" Arielle asked. "He had a global network with the Conclave, why didn't he just leave that open? And why wait until I came along?"

"It's localized…" V said. "There are areas of the map—at least from a contributor standpoint—that have always been blank. But what if the site is blocked in some parts of the world? Asia…Africa…South America? These places don't give us anything. What if there are people like Arielle with big portions of the star map already done?"

"The other people in my dream!" Arielle said. "They must have been other Star Prophets with different portions of the map. The senders were trying to get us to work together! That's what they meant by unite!"

"And whoever took down the map," V continued, "—and I still won't say it's Charles—already has the rest of the map? Or at least enough to get the idea of where Arielle's Ark is."

"Now this shady organization has the full map?" Max asked.

"I wouldn't want to know what they're planning on doing with it," Arielle said. "Do we even know what to do with it?"

"We send the message," V said. "We make our response and warn the senders before whoever took the map has a chance to contact them."

"Assuming they haven't already," Ryan said. "We also don't have the funding of a shadowy government force. How do we contact the aliens without a map?"

"We start over," Arielle said. "Ryan, you said that 'the Conclave's biggest asset has always been the other members'. We were close to our part of the map, maybe if we go around the official Conclave sites, we can get a more complete view of the map. Then, we send our own message and hope we call them first."

"How do we do that? Do any of you know Japanese?"

"We don't need to start from scratch," V said. "People have already started looking again. Old threads may be gone, but people are already organizing new ones."

"I think they'll come," Arielle said. "If they have the leadership of the Star Prophets."

"We're still starting from square one," Max said. "We don't have any of our old map to work off of…"

"Only partly true," V smiled. "I never gave Charles Algorithm 2.0 and it finished processing the other night. I compared it and it looked good. We lost the site, but not the map."

"The program in your room?" Arielle said. "You were reconstructing the whole map? I thought that was just visual white noise."

"I like to be thorough," V grinned. "Now, do we want to argue more about what to do? Or should we go and make contact?"

#

Looking at V's map felt like a weight had been taken off of Arielle's chest. They were no further along than when she last saw it, but the fact that they had a map again gave Arielle a newfound confidence that she could hardly believe. Things weren't as bleak as it had been a few hours ago.

"Arielle," Max said, dropping her bag on the kitchen table. "What do you want to tell the Conclave? Ryan and I can start spreading the message, but people would respond if it sounded like something you'd say."

"Tell them…" Arielle thought, rubbing her chin. "Tell them the Star Prophet is real. The map is real and we're going to rebuild it. Send the constellations to an email…a new one. We'll patch it through to Algorithm 2.0 and remake it ourselves. We can't trust the Conclave, but we can finish this together. The map was taken from us and we're taking it back. Our message goes out when we finish the map."

Max took dictation from the kitchen table on her laptop. Arielle looked over her shoulder for a minute, watching the message spread on all the major platforms, urging people to share it with other Conclave members or anyone who saw stars.

"V?" Ryan said, sitting on V's bed while they sat at their computer. "We're gonna need to run the constellations through your hardware. Can you automate the process and can your rig handle it?"

"It's not pretty," V said, typing out a new program on their computer interface, "but it's strong enough. I've been supercharging this hardware since before I was mapping stars. If a temperature warning comes up, I got a secondary cooling system we could kick on."

"V, can you help me with the transmitter?" Arielle asked. "I don't know enough about the pulse stuff you and Charles were talking about earlier."

"Yeah, shouldn't take long," V said, finishing the program for the algorithm. "What do you want the message to say?"

Arielle thought for a minute, took a slow exhaled and looked around the basement apartment. There was so much to say, but in a language that didn't translate to anything she wanted to express. "Let's do the transmitter first?"

"Deal," V said, rummaging through the cabinets next to their bed.

The next few hours were hard work. Arielle and V focused on the transmitter. Arielle usually just handed V components and tools when they asked for them, but was happy to be useful.

While they were working on the technical side of things, Max and Ryan were predominantly social. Max contacted her friend in Germany, getting his help in searching out the other Star Prophets. Ryan found a number of online threads relating to the star map and directed them all towards the new Conclave resources. The new Conclave was already sending new constellations to the updated algorithm and the system was processing dozens of new constellations a minute.

"Arielle!" Max yelled, making everyone jump. "I found one in South Africa!"

"What?" Arielle asked, sorting through screws for a specific size V was looking for.

"Another Star Prophet. She wants to see you face to face. I need you over here to confirm you're real."

"Go," V told Arielle before she could ask. "No offense, but you're kinda getting in the way at this point."

Max had already started the video call and Arielle straightened out her braids as the other caller picked up. On the other end of the screen was a slim, black woman with her hair piled onto her head in a bun.

"Star Prophet?" She asked in heavily accented English. "I have to say, I like your style."

"Call me Arielle. Arielle Walsh."

"Lydia Willis. Nice to know I am not losing my mind."

"You're another Star Prophet? Like me?"

"It started with a few constellations, but then it got out of control."

"What's your medium?" Arielle asked.

"Granny's yarn and buttons. She was not thrilled when I took over the living room with my project. I started submitting to the local site out here until it got shut down. Sounds a lot like your Conclave."

"Are you willing to send us your star map?" Arielle asked. "If we have different sections, it might speed up our efforts to rebuild the map."

"And send out a message? Consider it done. What are you going to tell them?"

"What would you say? I'm guessing you had the same dream…"

"*Unite*? Didn't make much sense at the time, but it helps now."

"Maybe they knew we were being blocked?"

"If it were me crafting that message? I'd want to meet them. You're the one who cracked the final piece of the puzzle, though. I leave it to you. I hope to hear from you when this is finished."

"Thank you, Lydia. I appreciate your help."

"Finish the map and share it when you finish. Maybe seeing the final product will make the constellations stop."

Lydia's face disappeared from the screen, Less than a minute later, Arielle could hear V's computer processing in the image that showed up in the email. After ten minutes of loud whirring, the computer finally settled and the star map doubled in size, Lydia's map appearing to the right of Arielle's portion.

"That's half done," Arielle smiled. She was a little teary-eyed to see so much of the map filled in. "Any leads on the others?"

"Based on the data we're currently getting?" Ryan started. "We're expecting someone in Japan and maybe Brazil. I'll work on those."

Arielle went back to work with V, but she mostly just watched as their transmitter came to fruition.

"We're not going to be able to send a long message," V said. "I want to repeat it a few times, but the shorter it is, the less that's gonna get lost in translation."

"Makes sense," Arielle said. "The messages to me have only ever been a word: 'Ark', 'Respond', 'Unite'…"

"So you're gonna need to be careful about what you say…"

"No pressure, though, right?"

"I'm not the one sending the message, Arielle." V grinned.

Ryan rushed over and grinned. "We found the Japanese Star Prophet. Toshi has been renewing the star mapper program basically by himself. He doesn't want a video chat, but I got three people translating for him."

"Three?"

"Japanese to Chinese, Chinese to Italian, Italian to English. Accounting for a few misspellings and translation hiccups? I think he's legit. He wants proof that you're real."

"Tell him we need to 'Unite'. Make sure that word goes through. It was a core part of the dream we shared."

"How do you know he had the dream?"

"I'm finding that with star mappers, two is enough for a pattern. Lydia had the same dream. I think that Unite is going to be the code word going forward."

Ryan typed out everything Arielle told him. There was a very long pause while Arielle assumed the other star mappers were translating. Arielle ruminated on what to say, but she was too distracted by the anticipation. After what felt like an hour, Arielle saw a notification pop up on Ryan's laptop. *Unite. Nice to know we aren't alone.*

"You told him everything?"

"He knows we're restarting the Conclave map over here. He just wanted proof you were who you were claiming to be before—"

V's computer started groaning again as the processors started going even faster. The map expanded again as a large collection of constellations appeared at the bottom right corner of the screen. It was processing smaller constellation clusters to fill in a few blank spots when Toshi's next message came through: *Tell them to please stay the heck away.*

"You think he really said that?"

"The Italian to English translator is a little too polite for my taste. Probably cleaned up the language a little, but they wouldn't change the main message."

"Regardless," Arielle nodded, admiring the screen, "we got another piece. We're close. Just need one more Star Prophet."

"Can we figure out where to broadcast from that?" V asked.

"No," Arielle shook her head. "I think the dream from the Senders was to ensure that we worked together Intentionally or not, we all had to share our knowledge with each other."

"I'm focusing on my contacts in Brazil. If we —"

"Not just Brazil, " Arielle cautioned. "Anywhere in that quadrant of the world. I don't want to miss something just because we were focused on our theory. It's good to focus, but we don't want to miss anything because we're over confident. We're too close to be careless."

The others agreed and the call went out to Central and South America. Arielle tried to help V, but the transmitter was finished. To keep herself busy, Arielle decided it was time to start considering what she wanted to send. While she would have wanted mankind's first message to the stars to be written on something grander and more majestic, all she had in her purse was a spiral notebook with a cartoon dog on the front. She couldn't even tear the page out because each corner was marked by the giggling dog's face. She filled entire pages with words, flipping through a dictionary and filling a trash can with discarded ideas.

"Got nothing?" Ryan asked, coming out of the basement and sitting on the stair next to her.

"It's so hard to pick just one word when there's so much I want to say. If we knew more of their language or had a more powerful transmitter, I might have a better message. Every word I can think of just...falls flat."

"Well, you're trying to pick one word out of millions. You could sit here for years and not find one word the completely encompasses everything you want to say. The part of your brain that let you fill out a big chunk of the star map? That's not meant for eloquent words or poetic word choice."

"Thanks?"

"What I mean, you shouldn't waste time trying to find the perfect word, but just the words you can think of. Don't try to find a big fancy word… pick the perfect Arielle word. Don't forget, they can only say one word at a time to us, too."

"Since when did you get so smart?" Arielle smirked.

"Chile!" V panted, popping their head out the door. "We found the last Prophet in Chile, we think."

"Think?"

"They reached out to us directly. He wants to see the rest of our map before he'll give us anything. The situation feels fishy…"

"I'll get to the bottom of it," Arielle marched into the basement and sat at the Max's laptop. She read the previous conversation that Max had been having with the mysterious user and focused on their word choice. She started typing her own message.

<<This is the North American Star Prophet. You're the Star Prophet from South America?>>

<<Seems to be the title I was given. Call me Andreas.>>

<<Can you prove you're not a fake? Are you willing to video chat?>>

<<No camera. Share your map and I'll share what I've got.>>

"Convenient," Ryan said, reading over Arielle's shoulder. "Still we took Toshi at his word."

"Toshi wasn't so weird about it," Arielle said. "This guy is really pushing a quid pro quo. Everyone else just wants to finish and wipe our hands of it —myself included."

Arielle started typing again. *<<What was the word the Senders gave us in our shared dream?>>*

<<Unite.>>

"Seems legit," Max shrugged. A funny feeling in the back of Arielle's head made her question him. Arielle typed again.

<<What color was my hair in the dream?>>

<<Blonde. Came down past your shoulders. I can send my part after—>>

That was all Arielle needed to close the conversation.

"That's not our guy," Arielle shook her head. "Block him…delete whatever thread he found us in. He's faking. None of us saw each other in our dream, just outlines."

"So, someone was trying to join our little game?" Max asked. "I don't like the sound of that."

"Who would fake being a Star Prophet?" Ryan asked. "How would they know about the word?"

"Unless someone spread it around? I think it's someone who overheard our private conversations. Besides, unless you were showing my picture around, they knew my face. That limits our suspects to everyone in this room…and Charles."

"Shit," Max swore, ruffling her curly hair. "Do you think he's trying to stop us?"

"Stop us, help us," Arielle shrugged. "Either way, he's hiding behind an alias. I want to see our next guy. Face to face only."

"I'll do my best," Max shrugged. "Sorry, Arielle, I didn't think someone would stoop that low."

"Ryan, help me with the coding on the transmitter," V said, plugging their tablet into the hodgepodge of pieces. "If we're this close, Arielle should work with Max to cut through all the noise. She's got a better sense of these things than you."

"Not gonna argue that point."

Arielle and Max sat back to back while skimming through messages from other star mappers and wannabe Star Prophets. Max's Spanish was better than Arielle's, but Arielle knew the best questions to quickly identify who was real or fraudulent. After three hours of searching and questioning, Arielle was waiting for the recipient in Mexico to pick up on her end.

She was a skinny girl with her dark hair tied back into a ponytail that she pulled through a green baseball cap. The room around her was dark, the screen making her face paler in the blue glow. For a moment, she was so still that Arielle thought the screen may have frozen. Max offered a quick greeting and the girl's expression shifted to a bright smile. She spoke quickly and Max translated as well as she could.

"I thought I was alone in this!" The other girl grinned. "Nice to find out I'm not crazy! I'm Maria."

"I'm Arielle. It's nice to meet you. You have another big part of the star map?"

"I think so, based on what you've been telling me. I've been stringing beads into patterns I didn't recognize for years! And then I started getting the dreams and—well, it's good to know I'm not alone."

"What was the word the Senders shared with us?"

Maria furrowed her brow when Max translated, but lit up again after a minute. "Oh you mean the Angels? *Unite.*"

"That sounds right," Arielle smiled. She had a better feeling about Maria already. "Are you willing to send us your part of the star map?"

Maria nodded, but frowned a little. Max started a quick exchange in Spanish, but Arielle could only make out the words for 'pictures', 'send', and 'help you'. Maria nodded and there seemed to be an agreement reached. She started talking again and Max nodded. "She'll send them to us as pictures from her phone."

"Send them in batches, if you can," Arielle asked. "We can get people here to process them and complete the star map."

"And then spread your message?" Maria asked. "Tell them we are waiting?"

"I haven't decided yet. There are people who wouldn't want them to visit."

"It isn't up to us, is it?" Maria shrugged. "I just hope we're ready if they do come."

"Thank you for your time," Arielle said. "Keep an eye on the message boards. We'll let you know what happens."

"Thank you, Arielle. I hope we all find what we're looking for."

With a smile, Maria waved goodbye and the screen went blank. Arielle's fists were clenched tight until the first batch of Maria's photos came through. It was beautiful beadwork that Max and Ryan worked together to convert into something useable for the new algorithm. Piece by piece, they uploaded each segment of the constellation. Max finished her pieces a little slower, but transferred the last of Maria's constellations to the algorithm. With all of the constellations uploaded, the Arielle and her friends watched the last pieces of the map spiral into place. As the last constellation snapped into place, Arielle could have cried with happiness when she saw the completed map.

"That is a thing of beauty," Max exhaled, laughing a little.

"OK," Ryan nodded. "Now what?"

"We send our message," V said, resolved.

"But where?" Ryan asked. "I don't understand this map. I mean, it looks great but…where does it begin or end?"

"We need an astronomer," Max said. "I mean, it'd be nice to know where we're supposed to be going…"

"Valkary's Breach…"

"What?" Max asked.

"I call them the Rings of Ryan," Ryan explained. "You call them The Fruit Loops and V calls them The Rings of Power. What about it?"

"We all see it," Arielle said, pointing to the sect of circles on the monitor. "Everyone—me, Lydia, Toshi, Maria?—we all see the rings on our section of the map. Everyone sees them at some point."

"It's a point we all share," Max nodded. "Either it's some kind of navigational device or it's our target."

"Given the fact that we don't know how to use their system?" Arielle said, "I'd bet it's the Ark. Now we just have to find ourselves."

"Too bad they don't have a North Star on here," Ryan sighed. "That'd make it a lot easier to figure out where we are."

"Maybe they do…" Arielle rubbed her chin. "V, do you still have that constellation you made like…three days ago?"

"Which one?"

"The gold club looking one? You were working on it just before your birthday party?"

V scrunched their face for a minute, but walked over to the other side of the apartment. They rummaged through a plastic bin, pulling out a dozen constellations made from wire and nuts before they found the one Arielle was talking about. V passed the constellation to Arielle, who took it and turned it in her hands. Adjusting V's lamp, Arielle shined light over the wire frame until the outline of the Big Dipper was silhouetted on V's wall.

Arielle spread V's constellation flat on the kitchen table and everyone gathered around to look at it from multiple angles. There was a frantic rush to the monitor display where everyone was looking over each other's shoulders until V triumphantly identified a spot on the bottom right corner of the map.

"I told you it was three dimensional!" V cheered.

"OK," Ryan said, looking carefully around the constellation, "but where's Earth?"

"Here!" Max pointed, setting her finger on the far bottom right corner of the screen. "Nine rings…if you count Pluto, that's supposed to be us."

Ryan took out his cellphone and typed for a few minutes while the others waited. "That's today…"

"What?" Arielle asked.

"I went to check the planet positions online? First hit that comes up matches with the positions that they're in now, give or take a few days! It's close enough that we can do it tonight."

"And we can use the Big Dipper!" V said. "That's a consistent anchor point in our solar system. There's a straight shot here…no stars or anything between our galaxy and the Ark."

"Why have all of this?" Max asked, gesturing at the remainder of the map.

"Maybe for other galaxies?" Arielle smiled. "We've been operating under the assumption that the map was only for us, but what if they reached out to any species who could hear it?"

"Wow…" V sighed. "I guess if you're reaching out to aliens, it's good to cast a wide net."

"So to recap," Ryan said, folding his arms. "We have our transmitter… we have our map…do we have our message?"

"I think so?" Arielle said. "We're gonna need to translate it, but I think it'll work."

"Well?" Max asked, sitting at V's table. "What word did you pick?"

"I went with 'Observe.'" Arielle said.

"Observe?" V asked. "Why that?"

"I thought it would be best not to invite them in or tell them to leave. I thought it would be best to just…tell them we heard them. They should come and observe our planet and then decide if they want to bother with us or not. I feel like our only obligation here is to let them know we heard. Maybe they'll follow up with request for more information, but we can least let them know we're listening."

"Diplomatic," Ryan said. "Besides, if there is another group out there who's trying to reach them, it would be good of them to come and observe before making any decisions. 'Observe' might be the safest thing they could do when it comes to us."

"Now we just need to translate," V said.

"How?" Arielle said. "I don't have an English to Sender dictionary…"

"It could be mathematical…" V rubbed their face and furrowed their brow. "Maybe you and I can work on figuring out what frequencies can be translated to words."

"You think we can just…guess their language?" Max asked. "That seems too easy."

"Since Arielle can understand their language," Ryan smiled. "I think she's the best equipped to decide how to do it."

Arielle let out a deep breath, looked to the map and grinned. "We'll never know until we try."

#

It took hours. Ryan left to get food for everyone and Max found a comfortable position on the bed for a nap. Arielle worked with V in the first moment of quiet they had. First, V and Arielle spent time with the words that Arielle knew: Ark, Respond and Unite. V played with sound waves played through the biggest set of headphones that Arielle had ever seen. Arielle focused as long as she could on a single word, feeling the frequencies the V was providing her with until she found three frequencies that sounded like they fit. The sounds seemed right, but it was hard to tell if that was how the Senders would receive the message. V's final pulse eventually tripped something in Arielle's brain that made her think of 'Observe.'

Ryan came back by the time they were finalizing the pulse, eating his burger silently while watching Arielle and V work. Even with their frequency in hand, Arielle still didn't feel confident enough in their pulse to start sending it out. She confirmed the frequency with Lydia and Maria, but Toshi was completely unreachable. The sun was starting to rise by the time they agreed that the signal was ready.

V was picking up the pieces of their transmitter and moving around the room with an energy Arielle didn't understand how they could have. "Ryan? You're with me."

"What?" Ryan asked. "Where?"

"Roof! We're gonna need a clear shot. My landlord probably won't notice…"

"Don't we need a big satellite dish?"

"Only if we're receiving radio waves as we understand them. We're just sending out a signal. The Senders gave us a time and date that we'll have a clear shot to the Ark. Now, come with me and help!"

V pulled Ryan out the door, slamming it behind them. Max snorted and woke up with a groan. Arielle took a pair of burgers out of the bag and handed one to Max, laying on the bed next to her. They chewed their sandwiches in silence, staring at the completed star map on the wall. When she finished her burger, Arielle approached the computer, emailed the complete star map to her phone and started posting it to every star mapper thread that she could find.

"You think that's smart?" Max asked. "The Conclave—the former Conclave will be able to see it."

"Let them," Arielle said, sitting next to Max and putting her head on her shoulder. "We already contacted them first. Besides, we're not sharing the language."

"That's true," Max folded her arms and rested her head on the top of Arielle's head. On the message boards, people were already calling Arielle's pulse 'The First Word of the Prophet.' Arielle couldn't help but feel proud. She and her friends had done it. Even if Charles and whatever organization the Conclave worked for was watching them, the pulse was only on V's personal computer. She doubted they were powerful enough to get it, but she knew they sent the first message anyways.

"—such a scaredy cat!" V laughed, opening the door to their basement apartment.

"I just don't feel super comfortable on third story roofs with nothing keeping me there." Ryan shook his head and reached into V's fridge, pulling out three beers.

"You should have seen him," V chuckled, grabbing their sandwich from the bag and tearing open the foil. "He was clinging to the chimney the whole time we were up there. His knees were quivering the whole time!"

"It was cold!" Ryan said, handing a beer bottle to Max.

Arielle took the bottle Ryan offered her and took a sip. She sat at kitchen table across from V and looked over at the screen. "You know something?" She said. "Looking at the completed map? This is the first time that I don't want to put stickers on my wall."

"I don't feel itchy either," V said. "When we finished the map, it was like the message was extra credit. We didn't need to, but I just wanted to."

"So, what do we do now?" Max asked, approaching the table. "Four years for nothing?"

"Not for nothing," Arielle said, folding her arms. "We made first contact with the Senders. That's enough for me."

"I agree," V said. "If they want to talk to us, we gave them the chance to see what they're dealing with first. Hopefully, we got to them before the Conclave."

"Do you think they'll ever respond?"

"I don't really care," Arielle said, taking a sip of her beer. She looked at the star map again and grinned. "We did what we set out to do. Now, all I want to do is appreciate what we did."

"We should still meet up," Ryan suggested. "Hang out…do non-Sender stuff. Our job is done. Now, we get our lives back."

V printed out copies of the star map for everyone. Arielle rolled hers up in a tube and went home on the bus, barely keeping her eyes open. When she made it to her apartment, she called out of work and slept for nine, dreamless hours.

After she woke up, Arielle put her completed star map on the one of the few open spots on her wall. Then, she moved her furniture back into her room and slowly took down each of her stars.

The Rebirth of Violet Franklin

The first of Violet's new memories was pain. It was a sharp pain, like a hot iron down the length of her spine. She wanted to call out and scream, thrash and escape. All she was able to do was moan weakly as the thunder faded into the distance. A form loomed over her, clad in green scrubs with a face mask.

"Violet? Vi?"

The deep voice was muffled, but familiar and warm. The gloved hand touched her face, the world blurring less as Violet was able to focus more on the masked man. His free hand went up and removed the covering over his mouth.

"Do you remember me, Vi? Don't speak yet! Just blink, if you can."

Violet concentrated and blinked, shocked by the effort it took. Her father smile, his white teeth shining through his bushy, brown beard. "Vi… you were in an accident. Do you remember that?"

Violet blinked again, a little stronger this time. Her breathing was stifled and she felt her own hot breath against her cheeks. The hot pain had dulled, but everything ached and it was hard to focus on anything as the pain wracked her body. It was worse than the wreck. The car accident had been violent, forcing the dashboard into her chest, but it had been over quickly.

"I had to do something, Violet," her father said. "I couldn't lose my beautiful flower. I know you're in pain now, but you will forgive me."

Violet's eyes focused more and she found an image above her. It took her a moment to realize it was her reflection. She whimpered hopelessly, looking at her face shrouded in bandages.

#

Days passed by too similarly for Violet. Her brief glimpses of consciousness came when her father had her eat and the half-aware state between sleep and fully awake. Soon, the periods of being awake were longer than the sleeping moments. By day three, she could flex her fingers. On day four, she could turn her head from side to side and see the other sides of the basement lab. After seven days, Violet's father helped her sit up and support herself upright on the edge of the table.

"Good, Vi," her father smile. "You're doing very well. Now, today, we're going to take off the bandages. I want you to remember that we've made great strides, no matter what. Are you ready?"

Violet nodded and watched her father come closer with a pair of scissors. The rasping cut of metal against the cotton bandages made Violet flinch until her father set the scissors aside and unwrapped her face. He smiled and touched her face. Violet took the mirror he offered and brought it up to her face. The face that stared back at her was stitched together from different shades of skin and one of the eyes in her head wasn't hers.

Her father explained everything over the following days. Simply, Violet had died. The car accident had killed her instantly. Her father refused to accept that fact. He was a brilliant surgeon with skills and resources. Her eye, it seemed, wasn't the only replacement.

Violet's brain and skull were hers and she had most of her original face. The right eye had been replaced. Most of her organs had been scavenged and restitched together. The skeleton had been made from other teenage girls her size, but the disgusting skin tapestry had come from anywhere her father could find it. Her fingers were mostly the same size, but the new hands felt clumsy. The pain she'd felt was a bolt of lightning that jump started her whole nervous system over again.

While she relearned how to use her body, her father would brush the long, brown hair until she could manage it herself. Violet did her best to walk, manipulate simple objects and talk again. Her father gave her gray sweatpants and a plain, white t-shirt to wear, offering fresh sets at the end of the day. It wasn't as if she was learning for the first time, but she was still struggling to build connections to the old, atrophied muscles that now moved her body.

"Where's—Mom?" Violet stuttered out, one day before dinner.

"Your Mom left. She couldn't stay after—well, I never gave up hope, Vi."

Violet's coordination improved each day. Soon, she was able to walk comfortably on her own and her speech was smoother than the first time she had croaked out words. Her father wouldn't let her near a television or computer, so Violet would spend time between meals reading.

Two weeks after her second birth, Violet crept out of the basement late at night. The windows were covered with sheets or boarded up like the house was condemned. Things were dusty and in total disarray. All of the family photos were removed from the wall. The house she'd grown up in now felt hollow and alien. It might have been because that's how she felt in her reconstructed body. She couldn't tell.

Violet's father was snoring loudly in his chair with a large book on his chest. She carefully snuck passed him and padded up the stairs to her old room. Her bed was covered with a big sheet and boxes were stacked in the far corner. Opening one of the boxes, Violet searched until she found her old computer.

Stepping back down to the basement, Violet closed the door without making a sound. Violet went to the mattress she'd been sleeping on since she could walk. She worked the keyboard carefully and typed her password with stiff fingers. Her social media accounts were still active, but most of the notifications were about how much she was missed. She'd been dead for six months.

Friends had wept. Abby, her friend since childhood, had been silent for weeks, but seemed to be active online again and moving on with her life. She found comfort in the small things, but Violet could still see the pain. Her boyfriend, Paul, was still very inactive, apart from monthly anniversary posts about how much he missed her. Her mother had deleted any social media accounts.

Her father's footsteps started Violet and she realized that it was time for breakfast. She hurriedly hid the laptop under her blanket just has her father came around the corner. If he noticed anything, he said nothing, but Violet could feel the laptop under her blanket. As she ate, she felt like he was staring at the lump under her left leg. When she finished her meal, they began their exercises for the day. After dinner, her father left Violet alone again and she took out the contraband laptop.

Violet looked up news on the car wreck. She and the other driver had died. It was hard to say who was at fault, but Violet did recall him coming around the corner too fast. A chill went up Violet's spine and she wondered if she had been remade with parts from the other driver.

After another hour on her computer, Violet couldn't stand it. She wouldn't be a prisoner. Her father had brought her back to life, but he couldn't keep her down her forever. She wanted to leave the dingy basement. The windowless walls were suffocating and she had a recurring nightmare that the door would vanish one day. She had to leave before her nightmare came true.

Violet snuck upstairs and put on an old, blue hoodie, musty from disuse. It covered enough of her face that she could get around with causing a riot. That was her hope, at least. Her sneakers felt a bit off, but she realized with nausea that it was because she had different feet now. Most of her other clothing fit, but the hoodie felt odd around her shoulders and her sweatpants were tighter on her right leg than her left.

With the hood pulled up, Violet went to the front door and undid the deadbolt. When it clicked open, she waited a long moment to see if her father would come running down the stairs. When she heard no footsteps, she unlatched the door and only opened wide enough to slip out into the dark.

It was fall already, the real world progressing faster than Violet realized. The leaves on the ground were brown and crisp, a thin later of frost on them. The big tree in the front yard was where Violet remembered playing in the summer, climbing up the branches until she could barely see the ground through the foliage. The small garden in front of the house had withered and died, long neglected since Violet's mother must have left. The night air was cool and Violet could smell a fire burning somewhere.

Violet's feet started moving, automatically walking down the driveway and turning left towards the wide circle of the cul-de-sac. At the house at the end of the road, Violet crept down the driveway and walked around to the backyard. Looking up, she saw Abby's light was still on.

"What would you even say?" Violet chided herself. "'Hey, surprise! I'm not dead anymore, wanna have a sleepover?' This is stupid...I should—"

A deep growl made Violet jumped. She'd nearly forgotten about the Rottweiler that Abby's parents had rescued when she and Abby were fourteen. Cautiously, Violet raised a hand and extended it to the dog. "Rowdy...come on, you remember me. Please?"

The big dog took a few steps forward, hackles raised and a low growl vibrating in his chest. He sniffed Violet's hand a few times, testing the scent and trying to recall it. Violet exhaled when Rowdy licked her hand and the little tail stub wagged.

"Oh, thank God." Violet wrapped her arms around Rowdy and let him lick her face. "I was so worried I'd lost myself somewhere."

"Who's out there?" Abby called from the porch. Her blonde hair was pulled back into a sleek ponytail and she was dressed in pajamas. She was armed with a bat, up over her shoulder in an attack position. "I'm warning you! Rowdy's a good dog, but he can bite!"

"Abby—"

"Rowdy, come!" Abby yelled. At the harsh command, Rowdy lumbered up onto the porch and stayed at Abby's leg. Abby looked back up at Violet. "Get out of her before I call the cops!"

"Abby, please…"

"How do you know my name? Why didn't Rowdy start barking? He hates strangers."

"I'm not a stranger…not entirely."

"Step into the light, slowly…with your hands raised!" Abby ordered, trying to hold the bat more menacingly.

Violet let out a breath and took a few, slow steps under the porch light, trying to use the shadow of the hood to hide.

"Where'd you get that sweatshirt?" Abby asked, pointing the bat at Violet's chest.

"I…trash can around the corner."

"Bullshit! That belongs—belonged to a friend of mine. Take it off and get out before I call the police!"

Violet did as Abby asked, trying to use her hair to hid her face. She tossed the sweatshirt onto the porch, closer to Abby than her. Violet folded her arms and tried to shrink into herself. Under the harsh illumination of Abby's flood light, it was impossible not to notice the stitches that held together her patchwork skin.

"Are you…are you okay?" Abby said, her caring nature overriding her fear.

"No…" Violet squeaked, trying not to cry.

Abby lowered the bat and took a few steps forward. She bent down and Violet made eye contact. "Holy shit," Abby exhaled, dropping the bat. "Violet?"

"I didn't — I wouldn't know how to — I just —"

Abby rushed forward and wrapped her arms around Violet, burying her face in Violet's chest, and sobbed. Violet squeezed back and shook from crying so hard.

"I thought you were dead," Abby cried. "They told me you were dead…"

"I…oh, Abby, I'm so sorry!"

"No," Abby took a breath and wiped her eyes. "You don't have to be sorry. We have to call your dad! He's been a mess since the accident and —"

"He knows."

"What do you mean?"

"He's the one who brought me back." It even tasted sour when Violet said it. "Can we talk inside?"

Abby nodded, taking Violet and Rowdy inside the house. Stepping through the back door, a rush of memories came back to Violet in a wave. Violet and Abby would watch scary movies in the living room. They'd nearly set the microwave on fire once and they had snuck in and out of the house using the lattice visible from the dining room. Violet's house was static and empty, but Abby's home was warm with what she remembered.

"Sorry about the bat, I just…when my dads aren't home I get spooked easily. Do you need anything? Water or — ?"

"No," Violet said, shaking her head. Without the sleeves of the sweatshirt to cover them, she was very aware of the stitched scars that held her body together. Abby say across from her with a big glass of water and took a few swigs. After nearly downing the water, Abby put the glass down on the table and relaxed her shoulders.

"OK," Abby exhaled. "What is going on? I thought you died in the car crash?"

Violet told her everything she could remember: the pain that had woken her up, the weeks of relearning to use her body, and all the time she'd spent hidden away in the basement. She told Abby about how isolating her father was and what little she knew about the things he had done to bring her back. Abby listening, pausing only to refill the glass and have another few sips of water.

"That makes some sense," Abby stood and grabbed a fresh glass from the cabinet. She filled it and offered it to Violet. "After the crash, I'd see your folks fight a lot. Your mom wanted to go to therapy, but your dad refused to leave the house much. By the time your mom packed up and left, your dad was a total recluse. I think I only ever saw him leave…once or twice in six months? And that was always at night when no one else was around."

"Why were you awake?"

"I don't sleep as much. Trauma nightmares that—well, lets's just say I'm glad to see your face."

"Even if it's not all mine?"

"It's still you in there," Abby affirmed. "Different parts of skin and your left eye isn't yours, but there's enough of the old Violet in your face to make me recognize you."

"So, my dad?"

"Right," Abby said, pausing to sip her water again. "Walter would go over there with baked goods all the time and Ben offered to help out with the garden when it started to go to shit. He would look away from me when I gave him a friendly wave. We were worried about him, especially after your mom left. I never assumed—I mean, I didn't think this was possible!"

"Neither did I." Violet hugged her shoulders. "I didn't think he would do it."

"Does he know you're not there?"

"No. He'd want me to stay down in the basement."

"And what do you want?"

"I don't want to go back there." Violet took a big sip of water and wiped her mouth with the back of her hand. "I mean, I don't know if I'd thank him for bringing me back, but I definitely don't want to spend the rest of my life in the basement."

"Then you won't have to. Walter and Ben will be back in the morning and we can talk to them then."

"They would help?"

"Well, I don't know the legality of it, but I don't think anyone will charge me with kidnapping if the person is considered dead."

"Grave robbing then?"

"Hey, you just told a joke!" Abby grinned a little. "I knew there was enough Violet in there!"

"Yeah," Violet grinned and raised her arm. "I'm in stitches."

#

"It's not the cleanest room in the house," Abby confessed, "but Brighton left for college and I didn't want the hassle of bringing my stuff up to the attic. Not visible from the street and not a lot of windows, but it's a step up from the basement, yeah?"

"It's more colorful, that's for—wait, Brighton went to college?"

"Oh, right, you missed that. He got accepted to URI about a month after your funeral."

"God, I really do have a lot to catch up on," Violet said. The attic room had a big bed with tie dye sheets, a large chest of drawers and a wardrobe painted red and gold. Above the bed, Brighton had nailed a big sheet to the rafters with little, paper cranes hanging from strings. Facing the bed were three easels with half-filled canvases on them. Violet and Abby would always hang out with her older brother while he worked on his paintings, listening to music and asking for his advice on navigating high school. That all seemed so far away now.

"Do you want me to stay up here tonight?" Abby asked. "The dads won't be home until morning and even then it's not weird for me to spend a night up here every now and again."

"I wouldn't mind the company," Violet sat on the bed. "Could I have my sweatshirt back?"

"Oh, of course!" Abby handed her the garment. "Sorry, I…does it hurt?"

"It did for a while." Violet pushed her head through the sweater and adjusted her hair. "Either it doesn't hurt as much or I'm just numb to the pain by now. All I could feel for the first three days was pain and—"

Violet wiped tears out of her eyes and took a shaky breath. The bed shifted as Abby sat next to her and put a hand on her shoulder. "We don't have to talk about it if you don't want to. I just wanted to know you were okay."

"I will be," Violet said. Adjusting herself, Violet settled onto the length of the mattress, softer and more comfortable than sleeping on the basement floor. Abby laid next to her and Violet rolled to look at her. "How's Paul?"

"He's still around. We spent a lot of time in the guidance counselor's office together. At first, school was…hard without you there, so teachers just let us study in the office together. Just friends, though. I would never—I mean, it's hard not to see him as anything other than your boyfriend."

"I wouldn't have blamed you if something happened, don't worry. Does he still play that flea market guitar we found?"

"He wrote your name on it in gold," Abby said. "Do you want him to —?"

"No," Violet spat and rolled to face away from Abby. "No one else can know about this."

"OK, I won't tell him."

"Abby? Could you hold me? My dad would barely touch me and I'm not fragile or anything. I just want—"

"I know," Abby moved closer, putting her arm around Violet's stomach. Violet reached up and touched Abby's small hand, enveloping it in her grasp. Violet slowly drifted to sleep while Abby ran her thumb over the rough stitches that connected Violet's hand.

#

"Violet? Violet, wake up!"

Violet inhaled deeply and looked around. She'd worried that she had dreamed her escape and that she was still trapped in the basement. Rolling onto her back, Violet looked up at Abby and memories of her get away came back in pieces. "Everything's okay. I just wasn't sure how to wake you up."

"What is it?" Violet asked, sitting up.

"My dads just got home. If you want to keep this a secret, then we need to hide you somewhere. If you want their help, we need to talk to them now."

Violet swallowed. The suggestion of involving Abby's parents was a good idea the previous night, but now it was harder to face. Violet closed her eyes and took a minute to think. Finally, she turned to Abby and nodded. "Better they find out on our terms than by accident."

"OK," Abby nodded, brushing some of Violet's hair behind her ear. "I'm gonna go talk to them. Stay up here, I'll be right back."

Violet got out of bed and walked to the wardrobe. Pulling it open, she found it was empty except for the mirror that was attached to the door. She looked herself over and frowned. She did what she could with her hair, pulling out the bedhead tangles and maneuvering it into a long braid that come to rest over her clavicle.

It made the scars more prominent, but Violet knew it would help Abby's dads see her for real. She hated the face that stared back at her in the mirror. The shape was hers, but the unfamiliarity of the new eye startled her each time she looked at herself.

"I don't see why we couldn't talk about this downstairs…" Violet heard Walter's voice as the family walked up towards the attic. Her pulse pounded so loud, she could feel it in her ears.

"It's something you wouldn't believe if I told you," Abby said.

"Abigail," Ben started, "what is so important that it can't—?"

Ben nearly fell backwards down the stairs when he made eye contact with Violet, but Abby took him by the arm. "It's okay. I know, I was startled, too."

Walter moved a little further up the stairs, but kept a wide berth from Violet when he saw her. Violet looked between the two of them and licked her lips. She wasn't sure what to say. Walter took a few steps forward, pushing his long dreadlocks aside. He was a tall man who could lift Violet and Abby over his shoulders on his worst day, but his hug was careful and warm when he wrapped his arms around Violet. Violet returned the hug, tears slipping down her face. Ben's arms folded around them both, his scratchy, dark beard on Violet's face.

"When we went to the funeral, we—" Ben stammered for the words. "I mean, we didn't think…"

"I thought it was a closed casket for the family's sake." Walter said, his big hands on her shoulders. "What happened?"

"It was my dad," Violet said, sniffling. "He did…something. I don't even know what…surgery or something unthinkable. He wouldn't tell me."

"We need to call Tom," Ben said. "It's his daughter, he has a—"

"He knew about this for weeks!" Abby said. "Violet ran away because she didn't want to be a prisoner in his home anymore! Pop, you have to let her stay, please…"

"It's the man's daughter, Abby!" Ben exclaimed, surprisingly angry. "If you ran off to someone else's house, I would want to know you're safe."

"But you wouldn't lock me in a basement," Abby said. "Please, she needs our help. Dad?"

"Ben?" Walter stepped forward. "Maybe we should listen to the girls. Tom has been acting strange…especially since Cathleen left. If we had known he was doing this—"

"We would have had him committed! I'm sorry, but regardless of his intentions—"

"Whatever he meant to do, he did it," Walter said. "Now, all that's left is to decide what we're going to do. Violet, do you want to go back to your father?"

"No." Violet shook her head.

"Then that settles it," Walter said. "Cathleen would want us to keep her safe. She can stay. If Tom comes looking for her, we can hash it out then. Until then, ignorance might be our best plan."

"Walter," Ben folded his arms, "this feels wrong."

"Not as wrong as I feel," Violet piped in. "He did things that I didn't think were possible. He unmade me and remade me…I don't even know how much of me is really me. I can't go back. Please, Ben…"

"Pop?" Abby asked, hopeful.

Ben rubbed his hand on his beard, moved his fingers up under his green cap and scratched his bald head. "Alright," Ben said. "Tom barely talks to us as it is. If he comes asking around, I'll play ignorance. I'm not familiar enough with this kind of family law, but I don't think there's a precedent here that we're violating. If the police get involved, I have to cooperate. That puts keeping this secret all on you colluders, understood?"

"So, she can stay?" Abby asked.

"She can stay," Ben sighed, resigned, "but I think we should call your mother. If not your father, you should be with a parent. I'm pretty sure you mom has more legal right than either of us do."

Violet nodded slightly. "I just need time to figure myself out first."

"You can stay in Brighton's room," Walter said. "Do you still…eat?"

Violet nodded with a smile, suddenly brightening. She turned and looked out the window, bright light pouring in through and making the bed glow. Violet had found a haven.

#

Violet picked at the fruit on her plate. She could handle a knife and fork easily enough, but her fine motor skills need practice. Picking up the individual blueberries was difficult at first, but Violet found that it was getting easier to perform basic tasks. She picked up a berry, she threw it in the air and opened her mouth. The fruit struck her forehead before it hit the floor.

"You still need to work on that, huh?" Abby asked, walking up into the attic with her backpack.

"In fairness, I couldn't do that before my rebirthday," Violet said. "School day?"

"Unfortunately," Abby said. "Neither dad says I can use the grief excuse anymore. You need anything before I go?"

"I should be alright," Violet said, pointing to Abby's laptop and a stack of books Walter had given her. "I got plenty to keep me occupied. Six months worth of news, social media stalking and TV shows to catch up on. Your dad lent me plenty to read: philosophy, religion, medical science, morality, ethics…"

"School is sounding preferable."

"I think he's trying to help me figure out…this." Violet motioned to herself.

"This isn't morality or philosophy, though. This is science fiction. When I get home? The works: movie marathon, popcorn, face masks—"

"It's gonna take more than a face mask," Violet smirked, pointing at the prominent scars on her cheeks. "I'll be fine. Go catch the bus."

"Dads are gone and you know where my bathroom is. Avoid the first floor…just in case. I'll be back at three!"

"Have a good day," Violet called after Abby as she rushed off to catch the bus. Popping a final blueberry into her mouth, Violet stretched a little and settled in with Abby's laptop for a day of catching up with reality.

#

Abby hopped off the bus and walked into school. She managed to make to her homeroom with five minutes to spare. Ms. Rogers perked up at her desk when Abby walked in and acknowledged her with a head nod. Abby took her seat near the back corner of the classroom. Paul rushed in, seconds before the bell rang.

"Photo finish, Mr. Monroe," Ms. Rogers said with a smirk.

"Well, don't you remember what you taught us about drama?" Paul grinned. "No tension means no plot."

"Mhmm," Ms. Rogers shook her head. "Happy ending this time, but predictability makes for boring plot. Take a seat before announcements start."

Paul sat, his spindly arms flopping and his chest heaving as he caught his breath. He brushed his shaggy, brown hair away from his face and exhaled. He was wearing a dark blue hoodie, a black t-shirt and jeans.

"So, no track, this year?" Abby asked.

"Har, har," Paul exhaled. "What's got you so chipper today?"

"Just in a good mood. Counselor James says I should embrace the good days when they happen."

"One for the books, then," Paul said.

The announcements started and Abby half listened to the droning voice of Whitney Vega over the speaker. Abby opened her notebook and started making a list of movies for tonight, focusing on anything Violet may have missed in the last few months.

"Hey," Paul leaned over to Abby and whispered, "want to study Briar's bio test this week? I am still super behind and could use a hand. After school today?"

"I can't. I got plans..."

"Plans? Since when did you have plans? With who?"

Abby tensed up for a moment and hoped Paul didn't notice. "She's someone I met at grief therapy…the group sessions you quit after a month?"

"Well, shit…I thought you hated everyone in group?"

"She's new. Just lost her dad."

"That sucks. Have you unloaded your personal trauma, yet?"

"Not yet," Abby said, relaxing her guard. "I don't divulge my dramatic backstory until level three of our friendship."

"Damn," Paul said, "only level three?" The bell rang and Abby slid her notebook into her backpack. Slinging her backpack over her shoulder and followed the herd of students shuffling out to their next class.

"Abby?" Ms. Rogers gestured, beckoning Abby over to her desk. "I know it's not in my official capacity as a teacher, but what is your relationship with Paul? You seem very intimate."

"Nothing serious," Abby urged. "Shared trauma breaks down a lot of barriers. We're just close friends."

"Most of my college relationships started as 'just close friends' and then evolved without realizing it. I know you've been struggling this year, but you don't have to restart your entire life and he seems to make you happy."

"It's complicated, Ms. Rogers. He and Violet were a very close couple. I was their third wheel for a long time and I'm comfortable there."

"It still feels like she's still around, huh?"

"You have no idea."

#

Violet ripped open the bag of chips and shoved a handful into her mouth. Her taste buds were shifting again and she was craving salt. Every so often, her desires changed and Violet would get strong cravings. Her father tracked these and tried to suppress them chemically so she could stay on an extremely strict diet. Now, Violet was relieved to be able to indulge in them.

Most of the morning, Violet searched for old friends, family and even a few teachers on social media. The world had turned in her absence, but Abby could help Violet fill in the blank parts of her timeline when she got home. Half a year's worth of news was a lot harder to take in over breakfast, so Violet focused on the biggest news stories and a couple local papers. It was still too much for to process in one session of of reading.

Violet spent some time practicing walking. While it was becoming more natural, the repetition of using her new muscles made it easier to keep her balance. Manipulating objects with her hands was still difficult, but she was able to use the pen better as she took more notes. When Rowdy huffed at the base of the stairs, Violet walked down and threw a ball down the hallway for the muscular dog to chase. Her father's exercises were helpful when she was getting acquainted with her new muscles, but practical use felt almost normal.

A car ignition went off in the driveway. Violet tensed. It was barely noon and no one was supposed to be home yet. Violet climbed up on the bed and peeked out through the window at the peak of the roof. She knew the red sedan and saw her father's grey head as he stepped out of the driver's seat. Violet tensed as someone knocked on the door, setting Rowdy barking.

Violet rocked back and forth, holding her knees close to her chest. "He won't come in," she whispered to herself, "he won't come in, he won't come in, he won't—"

"Hello?" Her father's voice called from the front door. "Anyone home?"

"He won't come in," Violet repeated to herself, wrapping her arms over her head. "He won't come in, he won't come in…"

Violet was still shaking when she heard the car door open and close again. The sedan started up and the rumble of the engine faded down the street. Violet's breathing was quick and uneven as she tried to settle her mind. She had to force her thoughts away from visions of her dad breaking the door down, running up stairs and dragging her back down to the basement. Opening her eyes, Violet focused on what was real. "The tie dye blankets, the sound of birds, the small of paint, the softness of the blankets, the salt on my lips. I am real. This is real. I am real…"

With a deep breath, Violet unclenched her rebellious muscles and leaned back on the bed. Violet could feel her pulse slowing as she took a few more deep breaths. The world seemed to relax a little and she didn't feel like she was going to throw up anymore.

"Damn it," Violet exhaled. Despite everything, she hadn't had a proper panic attack since waking up. Her mother had taught her how to grasp reality when she was young, but she hadn't used the technique in a while. The fact that thinking of her father had caused a panic attack wasn't a good sign.

Sitting up again, Violet closed the laptop and took one of the books off the bedspread. Taking one of the thick blankets off the bed, Violet curled up in a nest, cracked the book open and hid in the words of medical science, trying to understand exactly what had happened to her.

#

Abby stepped off the bus and adjusted her backpack on her shoulders. She couldn't wait for Brighton to come home from college so she could have a car again. Still, the bus was faster than walking. Stuffing her hands in her denim jacket, Abby nearly jumped when the red car slowed beside her.

"Dr. Franklin?"

"Abigail," Violet's father smiled awkwardly. "Good to see you."

"Nice to see you out and about. I haven't heard from you since —" Abby stopped herself and looked down.

"No need to beat around the bush. What happened is in the past. How—has school been going well?"

"School?"

It's just I, uh…never mind."

"Is everything alright?"

"Oh, just longing for normality after so much has changed. I just wanted to be sure you were alright."

"Of course," Abby nodded. "I hope to see you again soon."

"It's good to see you again, Abby. Seeing you…it brings back better memories. You and Violet were so close. It's nice to see you recovering from tragedy."

"Dr. Franklin?"

"I apologize," Dr. Franklin said. "Take care, Abby. It's good to see you again."

Dr. Franklin waved a hand and drove off down the road, turning away from the cul-de-sac. Once he was out of sight, Abby leaned forward and dry heaved into the bushes. She wasn't a good liar, but she didn't think Dr. Franklin noticed anything odd. Tucking her hair behind her ears, Abby continued walking down the street, nearly running when she could see her house. Abby cleared the steps in a quick jump, opened the door and slammed the deadbolt into place once she was inside. Dropping her backpack, Abby slowly moved up the stairs. Violet was asleep in the beanbag in Brighton's room with a book open on her lap.

"Hey Violet…" Abby reached out and squeezed Violet's shoulder. Violet groaned and blinked a few times, stretching towards the rafters with a weak smile.

"What's wrong?" Abby asked. "You're doing that fake smile thing."

"My dad came around earlier today," Violet said. "He knocked on the door and left shortly after that."

"He stopped me when I got off the bus. He was still…weird, but was just asking about school."

"He knows I'm not in the basement. He knew I'd come here first."

"Why didn't he just break in?"

"He's smart. He knows if he's caught, he'll go to jail and then he'll never find me. He's playing the long game, he knows he can."

"Which is a special kind of terrifying," Abby said. "We're gonna be safe, I promise."

"I can leave…"

"No, you can't," Abby said. "Not yet. Let's get the whole thing out of your head, alright? He left the neighborhood and he's not getting inside the house. I have a list of movies you've missed and managed to get a bunch from the library. Our only concern right now? Do you still eat popcorn?"

"I've been craving butter…" Violet smiled.

The pair set up in Abby's room, projecting the movie onto a blank wall opposite her bed. Rowdy stretched out between them and set his big head on Violet's lap. The first movie was a light comedy, but Violet wasn't paying much attention to the plot, laughing more at the situational humor than anything. Between movies, Abby went downstairs at one point to talk with her dad and returned with a steaming box of pizza.

"I love your dads," Violet said, taking the first slice. "My dad had me on a very strict diet. Steamed vegetables and bland meat. Pizza was off the menu entirely."

"Well, that's just criminal," Abby laughed. "Have you figured everything out that you wanted to?"

"Well, technically speaking? I am conscious and aware enough to be considered alive. I still feel like myself, but it's hard to argue if I'm still the old me, since there hasn't been a brain transplant to make that argument before. Certain philosophies suggest that self goes beyond physical brains and thought. However, all the organs aren't me and that's supposed to be a part of who we are too. Medically, the physical body is hormones, muscles, blood flow—in addition to the mental processes of thought."

"Profound," Abby said, "so what do you think about the new you?"

"I'm still Violet. You're still my best friend. Everything else is fuzzy. I had a panic attack today, so that's still the old me."

Abby nodded and chewed on the crust of her pizza. "Do you wanna call your mom tonight?"

"Not yet," Violet said, rubbing her arms. The stitching on her hands snagged on the stitching up her arms. "I've been dead for six months and—it would be too much for her to know all of this now. There's no guidebook for reintegrating a dead person back into society. Even if this was all legal—which I doubt—would people even accept...me?"

"I do."

"Really?" Violet pointed at her scared face.

"I mean, it was a shock at first, I won't lie. But you're still my best friend and I'm sure Paul would—"

"No," Violet snapped. "Not Paul. My mom eventually, but Paul is...off limits."

"Vi—"

"He deserves a normal life...even if it is without me. He should have a girlfriend...go to college...get married—"

"So do you," Abby said. "Every weekend he goes to your grave. He still wears the shirts you gave him and keeps that concert ticket from your first date in his wallet. You want him to have a normal life, but he will never stop loving you."

"But will he love...new Violet?" Violet asked.

Abby opened her mouth, but stopped. She reached out and took Violet's hand, running her fingers over the scars. "I think we should call your mom."

"I know. It's the only way I can really get away from my dad."

"Tonight?"

"Tomorrow," Violet confirmed. "After you get home from school. I feel like I'm gonna need a day to figure out what to say."

Abby nodded and started the next movie. Violet found it impossible to concentrate on the film, weighed down by the ever tightening knot in her stomach.

#

Violet couldn't remember the last time she properly dreamed, but she was dreaming now. She was in her car again, sitting behind the wheel and wrapping her fingers around the top of the wheel. She glanced up in the rearview mirror and was startled by the stitched up reflection looking back. The windshield was suddenly enveloped by bright, white light that filled her vision moments before she—

Violet managed to bolt up awake before the impact. She focused on the reality around her, physically gripping the sheets until her knuckles burned. Slowly, Violet unclenched her fingers and relaxed. She'd woken up in time. Of all the memories her brain could come up with, she had to dream about her accident. She wasn't sure she could sleep anymore tonight.

Climbing out of bed, Violet padded across the floor at looked at herself in the wardrobe mirror again. She was getting used to her new appearance, even if it did still make her uncomfortable to look at. It was wrong and unsettling. The stitches never popped or ruptured. They were waterproof and never frayed or broke. Violet wondered if her father had ever intended for them to be removed or if she was to be a living testament to his genius.

Violet had always believed her father was a good person. How could her father—the man who'd raised her—do something like this? He was the best surgeon around, known for doing an eight hour heart transplant without stopping or even taking a break. There had been a complication in the middle, but Dr. Thomas Franklin refused to let that boy die on the table. When the parents weren't able to pay for the emergency surgery, Violet's father made sure the hospital only charged them for the initial surgery. He told reporters later that no human life could be condensed to a dollar amount.

Violet figured he'd thought the same of her. How much had he spent on her organs? The skin? How many hours had he spent stitching her together? What was the cost of her second life?

Brushing the thoughts from her mind, Violet closed the wardrobe and went to lie down in the bed again. Her waking thoughts didn't need to drive her to guilt. Her father may had committed a crime. Each of her organs was meant for someone else. The thought of the number of lives her father had ended made her want to vomit.

#

"Hey Abby…"

Abby looked up from her lunch, surprised to see Paul. He looked exhausted and haggard. "Rough night? I didn't see you in homeroom."

"Didn't sleep," Paul sat across from her. "Our song came on the radio and I spent most of the night…never mind. Can I borrow your English notes?"

"Yeah," Abby said, taking out her notebook.

"You haven't missed class in like…two days."

"So?" Abby asked. "What's weird about that?"

"No, it's just—I don't know how you can be over it."

"Paul," Abby sighed, "there's no magical 'it' you need to get over. We have good days and bad days when it comes to grief. I've just…had a few good days."

"'Cause of your new friend?"

"What's that supposed to mean?"

"Come on," Paul scoffed. "You don't feel a little guilty?"

"First of all," Abby snarled, "I don't see how feeling guilty changes anything about what happened. Secondly, if you're implying I'm trying to replace Violet with someone else, you're an idiot. What's got you in such a good mood, dick?"

"Whitney asked me out and I just…locked up. I felt like bursting into tears because I just thought I'd lose her, too."

127

"Paul…"

"I still have dreams she's alive, you know?" Paul asked, his voice breaking. "I'll be with her and I'm so angry when I wake up again. I never got to say goodbye to her. I thought I'd see her the next morning and we'd go get lunch. I just didn't think that she'd — I should've — it's not — "

"Paul, breathe…" Abby said, putting a hand on his forearm. "I know it's hard, but we can't live our lives for someone who's gone. She'd want what's best for us."

"I keep going back to her grave." Paul wiped his eyes, wetting the back of his hand. "And the therapist said it's supposed to help, but I just feel empty. I feel like I'm just talking to empty space."

"I think she'd want you to move on," Abby said. "You're allowed to have a life, Paul. She wants you to be happy."

"You're right," Paul nodded. "I just miss her."

Abby swallowed and nodded. "I have to go to class…and so should you."

Paul nodded, but Abby still felt like his stare was too vacant. She set a hand on his shoulder as she walked by and he looked up. "She loved you, too. Now, go to class…"

#

"It was…" Violet said aloud as she wrote, *"painful to wake up…and see what Dad had — "*

Frustrated, Violet tore out the page from the notebook, crumpled it her hand and threw it into the pile by the trashcan. Letting out a deep breath, Violet started again.

"Mom…" Violet thought for a moment and revised the beginning. *"Dear Mom…you deserve to know* — know what? I don't even know!"

Rowdy perked up at the sounds of Violet's frustration, putting his big head on her right leg. "Sorry, bud," Violet sighed. "There's no resources for writing a letter like this. With Abby, it just kinda happened, but I can't just stumble into this with my mom. And I don't know if I could video call that would…what would she think?"

Violet flopped on the bed and rubbed the spot between Rowdy's ears when he adjusted his head to her stomach. "Then again…showing her might be the only way to convince her. Would she take me anyway? I don't even know where she is."

"Hey," Abby said, as she clomped up the stairs in her heavy boots. "Projecting personal insecurity on the dog again?"

"It's a classic staple. Not my fault Rowdy is a better therapist than my parents…or you."

"I'd be offended, but he is a much better listener. If it helps, I can talk to your mom first? Kinda…prepare her for it?"

"OK," Violet fixed her hair a little, tidying the two braids on either side of her head. "Let's do it."

"You sure?" Abby asked, looking at the pile of crumpled paper. "We could work out something useable together, if you wanted to."

"I spent all day trying to find the perfect words. There aren't any. I think we just need to…jump into it."

"OK," Abby took out her phone and found Violet's mom in her contacts. "Let's hope she still has her old number…"

The screen rang a few times, the automated tones making Violet more nervous each time it sounded. Abby sat next to Violet and angled the phone so that Violet wouldn't be seen. Before long, it stopped and was replaced by the sounds of a hand passing over the microphone.

"Hello?"

"Mrs. Franklin? It's Abby."

"Abby? How are you, sweetie? Is everything alright?"

"Everything is…well, how are you?"

"Do you need me to call your dads? What's going on?"

"Well…you should sit down first."

"Abby, what's — ?"

"Just…please sit down."

There was a moment where Violet heard the sound of her mother's heels on the hardwood floor of a big, empty room.

"Abby, what's going on? Are you in trouble?"

"There's something I need to tell you, but I don't know how to say it. The easiest way is just…showing you."

"Why aren't you calling your dads?"

"It concerns you more than them. Promise you won't freak out?"

"Why?"

Abby looked to Violet. Violet nodded and took the phone from Abby. Violet felt like she could taste the bile in her mouth as her face appeared in the small corner of the screen. There was a brief moment of recognition before Violet's mom brought her hand to her face.

"Hi, Mom…" Violet grinned. Violet's mom's phone fell to the floor and clattered hard against the hardwood.

"Should…" Abby frowned a little. "Do we call her back?"

"Mom?" Violet pleaded to the empty screen. "Mom!"

"I'm here, I'm…Violet is that — no, it's not possible! I was there when we had to — why do you have my daughter's face?"

"Mom, it's me…it's Violet. I broke my arm freshman year playing softball when I swung too early and shattered my wrist. When I was fourteen, I begged you to let me get a puppy like Abby's, but you refused because you thought Rowdy was…uh, 'a drooling mess' that you'd be stuck with after I left for college."

"You had a recurring nightmare when you were six…" Violet's mother said, fighting to keep her defenses up. "You made me swear never to tell anyone, not even Abby. What was it?"

"I—I dreamed that I drowned in Abby's pool because Brighton pushed me in at her birthday."

"Violet!" Violet's mom cried, tears slipping down her cheeks. "Oh my… how are—how is this possible?"

"It's Dad," Violet said, choking on her own tears. "He's not right, Mom. Something is wrong."

"The bastard did it…"

"Did what?" Violet asked. "You knew about this?"

"When I left your father, he was…manic. He didn't sleep, he barely ate and he only ever spoke about this grand revelation he was working on. He said he'd have you back. I tried to talk him out of it, but he was too far gone. I didn't have any evidence that he was breaking any laws, so I couldn't get him arrested. I left before he could—it was hard for me to do, Violet. If I'd known he was going to do this, I would have tried harder to stop him, but —"

"It doesn't matter." Violet shook her head, fiercely. "I just…I want to go, Mom. I want to get away from him."

"I'll be there as soon as I can."

"Where are you, by the way?" Abby asked, poking her head into the picture. "We saw you just…leave one night and no one in the neighborhood knew where you went."

"Actually, I asked for a transfer to corporate in my company…in New Jersey."

"New Jersey?" Violet asked, like the word left a bad taste in her mouth. "Why did you go to the armpit of New England?"

Violet's mom laughed through her tears, wiping her eyes. "Now I know you're still my daughter."

"How soon can you get here?" Violet asked. "I can't go back to the old house, Mom…"

"I'm trying to find flights now…" Violet's mom set her phone down and typed furiously on her computer keyboard. I can probably catch one at nine in the morning, but that would get me to you in the early evening at best."

"Whatever it takes," Violet said. "Can I go back with you?"

"Sweetheart, of course."

"The only problem might be getting her a ticket," Abby said, suddenly practical. "Violet has no ID that can prove she's who she says. And that's ignoring the fact that she's still considered dead by the state."

"We can figure out the legal stuff while I'm there, but I'm sure you're not the first person who needed their death certificate voided."

"Certainly the first like this…" Violet grimaced, looking at her hand and showing her mom the scars. "I should have called sooner, I'm sorry. I just… didn't know how to tell you."

"You're alive," Violet's mom let out a shaky breath. "We'll figure the rest out tomorrow…or the next day. I'll be on the earliest plane out of here in the morning."

"I'll…well, I don't have anything to pack."

"Are you at the Greens' house?"

"Yes, up in Brighton's room."

"I'll call Walter and have him leave a spare—"

"No!" Violet urged. "Don't come to the Greens'! Dad's been skulking around. I think he's trying to find me and if you suddenly come to the old neighborhood, Dad will get suspicious. We need to meet somewhere else."

"I'll book a room in a hotel…the one off of Exit 45."

"I know the place," Abby said. "Benjamin can help us smuggle her out of the garage and then help with the legal stuff."

"I'll be there."

"Mom, I'm…I'm sorry."

"Don't be. We'll be together soon and we'll be on the first flight we can get. I love you, Violet, no matter what."

"I love you, too. I'll see you soon."

Violet hung up the call and burst into tears. Abby rushed over, cradling Violet's head against her chest and running her fingers through her hair. Violet sobbed, feeling like she could breathe for the first time since she'd been brought back. It was almost over.

#

"And you can have these…" Abby threw a few t-shirts on the bed. "And these…that top has always looked better on you than me anyways. Try on these pants to see if they fit."

"I'll bring it all back, I promise," Violet said. "I just need something until we can figure out how to get all my stuff back from my dad."

"Benjamin and your mom will figure out the legal way. If not? Walter and I will go rob the place. You know I look best in black."

Violet laughed and tried on the pants Abby offered. Abby's phone buzzed on her dresser and she picked it up. Her smile faded.

"What's wrong?"

"Nothing. Paul texted me."

"Did you tell him?"

"No, of course not. He's having a really rough week. We've been relying on each other for support. We were in a grief group together for a bit, but it just made him angry. I think he's still doing private therapy, but I don't know how often. Mostly he just…asks for my notes when he skips class."

"He's not good, huh?"

"No," Abby said.

There was a heavy silence in the room as Violet tried on the jeans. They felt a little tighter around her right leg than her left, but that was something Violet was getting used to. It wasn't constricting and she could still walk.

"Not for nothing?" Abby said, swallowing. "Paul feels guilty he wasn't with you that night. He blames himself. I'm not saying you have to get back together with him, but he needs closure."

"Abby—"

"You're going to New Jersey with your mom, right? That's on the other side of the country and he may never get the chance to see you again. Are you really gonna deny him the opportunity?"

"I'm scared, Abby, alright?" Violet yelled, louder than she meant to. "Is that what you want to hear? I'm scared he's gonna look and me and see—well…me."

"He won't care about that," Abby said. "He goes to your grave all the time. He thinks he's talking to you, but he's just spilling his guts to a headstone. And he knows, in his heart, that it's empty. I'm not saying you have to do anything, but…let him say goodbye."

"And then break his heart by leaving him again?"

"I think he can feel you're not really dead."

"God, you are such a romantic sap," Violet sighed, checking over herself in one of the t-shirts.

"I'm just saying, if I had the chance to say goodbye when I heard you died? I would have had a much easier time sleeping."

"What do you mean?"

"I—I should have been in the car with you, but I…I don't even remember why I didn't go with you."

"You left early. You needed to take care of the dog and got a ride home from Avery."

"Right," Abby shook her head, shaking off cobwebs, "but we were supposed to go home together."

"Abby, this wasn't your fault."

"I know that now, but for months I couldn't sleep because I'd have nightmares that I was the one who was supposed to die. And maybe I would be able to sleep again if I wasn't wrecked with guilt for months after you died."

"Abby—"

"For Paul's sake…let him say goodbye to you."

Violet exhaled slowly and rubbed her forehead, careful to avoid the stitches around her eye. "Okay."

"Okay?"

"If it will help him move on, he can come over tomorrow after school before we go to my mom's hotel. But you can't guilt me into anything until we get my family life sorted out!"

"I won't, I promise!" Abby brightened. "I'll let Walter and Ben know and then text Paul."

The knot in Violet's stomach returned, heavy and leaden.

#

The knot remained in Violet's gut through the next morning. She hated not knowing what was happening. It was all nerves and every technique that she knew of to try and set herself back in reality. Before she died, she would text Paul and he would help slow her brain down. Now, she listed everything she could see, feel and hear until Abby came upstairs.

"Hey," Abby said, delicately. "So, Paul and I will be back after school. He doesn't know he's coming to see you, yet. I just told him I'd help him get closure."

"Thanks."

"But as one friend to another? It might not hurt to shower…"

"Thanks," Violet laughed a little. Abby didn't say anything, but Violet listened to her walking down the stairs. After a few more minutes in silence, Violet sat up and looked around the chilly attic. She would be done with all of this soon. Each loose end was starting to wind together into a single rope.

Violet would be with her mom soon. There had to be a way to get her away from her father, either by getting out of the state or putting him in jail. She could get a new identity if that's what it took. She could take online classes and get a job. Before she called her mother, Violet hadn't considered striding into the future the way she was. Now, she had a plan. the only tie left to cut was Paul.

Climbing out of bed, Violet padded down the stairs and into the bathroom. If she was forced to meet Paul, she could at least look presentable. She wondered about putting on some of Abby's makeup, but stopped herself with a laugh. "Like putting new paint on a burning train…"

Violet undressed and turned on the water, hot steam filling the cold bathroom. Standing under the shower head, Violet let the water soak her hair and back before stepping away from the stream to use the soap. The stitching was rough and unnatural as her fingers grazed the seams the held her body together. Long sleeves, Violet decided, would have to be her new normal.

After rinsing off, Violet dried herself with a towel and started brushing out her hair. When that was finished, she left the bathroom wrapped in a towel and got dressed. She settled on a pair of jeans, a black, long-sleeve shirt and flat sneakers that Abby had let her borrow. Opening the wardrobe, Violet tried to figure out how wear her hair to meet a boyfriend from a past life.

Violet settled on leaving her hair loose. It wasn't the stringy mess it had been when she first came to the Greens' house and wearing it down would cover more of her scars and made her feel more confident. With that finished, Violet sat on the bed next to Rowdy and flipped through a book about medical ethics. In her heart, she knew she'd be rereading the same page for the rest of the day.

#

"Abby, what is going on?" Paul's deep voice was muffled through glass window to the outside, but Violet could still recognize it. "I thought you meant we were going to visit Violet's grave or something. I'm starting to wonder if you used me for the free ride. Are we gonna bust out the ouija board?"

Rowdy perked up when Violet tensed on the bed, then bounded off the bed and rand downstairs to protect the household. Violet tasted bile and got off the bed, pacing the room to try and settle her nerves before a panic attack took over. She heard the front door open and Rowdy barked loudly.

"Down, Rowdy!" Abby said, sternly. The Rottweiler settled and Violet heard Paul's soft voice speaking to the dog. Rowdy settled. Violet did not.

"Trust me a little," Abby said, the sound of the feet on the stairs coming closer. "Just…wait here for a minute, OK?"

Abby's head popped up and looked around. Violet stood near the beanbag behind the canvases, gripping her shoulders. She rocked a little until Abby came over. "I'm right here," Abby whispered, putting her hands on Violet's shoulders. "You're safe, I promise."

Shaking, Violet closed her eyes and took a deep breath. She opened her eyes and nodded steadily to Abby. Abby walked over to the stairs and walked down to lead Paul up.

"Just don't freak out, okay?"

"I can't make that promise until you tell me what's—"

Paul stopped at the top of the stairs when he saw Violet. Violet swallowed and walked through the maze of canvas paintings into the brighter sunlight. She did everything she could to hide her face, but she couldn't look away from Paul's shocked eyes. "Hey, troublemaker…"

"Vi?" Paul stammered out, finally. "No, this…this isn't real."

"Paul," Abby steadied him with a hand. "I didn't believe it at first, either. You know her almost as well as I do. You have to see her."

"No, Violet—Violet is dead."

"I was." Violet swallowed, suddenly sweating and itchy. Paul took a few steps forward and looked at Violet's stitched face intently.

"Can I—?" Paul asked, lifting his hand towards her cheek. Violet nodded and led Paul's hand to her face, trying to avoid the thickest knot of stitches around the eye that wasn't hers. Paul's hand was warm and clammy, but Violet pressed her cheek against his palm. It was a small touch, but it was so human. Violet closed her eyes as Paul's hand reached up and pushed some of her hair back behind her ear. Putting her nose to his wrist, Violet inhaled deeply and looked up at Paul. It smelled like the cologne she got him for Christmas when they started dating.

"Violet?" Paul smiled. "How did…why would you fake your own death?"

"It wasn't a fake, Paul." Violet said. "I did die. The funeral was real. All of this? That was my dad."

"Your dad?"

"I'll give you guys a few minutes," Abby piped in. "Take all the time you need."

Abby rushed downstairs and Violet stood across from Paul, his hand still in Violet's hair. Violet stepped away and sat on the bed, motioning for Paul to join her. Hesitantly, Paul sat next to her and gripped his hands on his lap.

"What—?" Paul stammered. "I mean, how are you here?"

"It's a long story," Violet said. "My dad did it. I don't know how but…I don't know if I could explain it if I knew."

"Does it hurt?"

"Yes? No? It kinda hurts, but it's an ongoing pain that I've felt since waking up."

"I'm sorry."

There was a brief moment when neither said anything. Violet ran her thumb over the scars on her left hand, her nail snagging on each thread. She let out a breath in the silence. "Abby said you've been skipping class?"

"Some days are better than others," Paul said.

"And you stopped going to therapy?"

"It doesn't work for me."

"Paul," Violet pleaded, firmer. "You need to to let me go."

"What? I just got back and now you're telling me I need to forget you?"

"Paul—"

"No! You were the most important person in my life and when you were gone I…" Paul cursed and looked down at the floor. "I'm not blaming, but I don't want to lose you again."

"Paul, look at me," Violet said. "Look at me." Paul looked up from his sneakers and looked at her. "I'm not who I used to be."

"I don't care about that, Violet. I want to be with you."

"All the stitches?" Violet pulled up her sleeves and displayed the patchwork skin up to her elbows. "It's not just my face or hands. It's everything. As far as I know, only my brain and skull are mine anymore. Everything in me was meant to be someone else's."

"I don't care."

"You say that, but you can't even look at me."

"It's not the rest of you I can't look at. Looking you in the eyes isn't easy. I hurts to know how hard I was trying to move on. I gave up on you, Vi…"

"I'm not blaming you," Violet shifted and put her hand on Paul's knee. "I'm giving you permission to move on. I need you to find someone else."

"I don't want someone else," Paul said. "I wanted to marry you. And the thought of anyone else is painful."

Violet reached up and turned Paul to face her. Touching her forehead to his, Violet took a deep breath and set a hand on the base of his neck. Paul's breathing matched hers and he brought his hand up and pushed his hand into Violet's hair. He held her for a moment, the world drowned out by their unified breathing. "We can be together again, Vi…"

"I'm going to live with my mom. With everything that happened here, I can't stay so close to my dad."

"I could date long distance."

"Paul, I'm serious…"

"So am I," Paul said. "Violet, I still love you. I miss you everyday. When I skip class it's because I can't think of going in without seeing your face. I still bring you coffee on Friday mornings and I almost punched someone for sitting in your chair a month after the funeral. And now that I know you're here? I can't do that again."

"It's not fair to you."

"It wasn't fair already. I won't make you stay or do anything you don't want to…but don't make me give you up again."

Violet rand her hand through Paul's hair and chuckled. "I could kiss you, you idiot."

"I wouldn't stop you."

"I'm not staying in town," Violet said.

"I can go out to…where, exactly?"

"New Jersey."

"That's a long flight, but I could do it to see you. And there are schools in New York I could look into when I graduate."

"I can't promise that I'll be who you want anymore."

"We can find out together, but I still knew it was you. Not your face or your eyes. It was how you stood and the way you looked at me. I can still see you through everything."

Violet took Paul's free hand and brought it up to her face where she knew there were more stitches. Paul shivered a little, but the tension in his hand relaxed and stroked her cheek with his thumb. "This is what I am now. I'm not who I used to be, Paul."

"Violet, I told you why I loved you a long time ago. It wasn't your face or your hair or—if I can be frank—great ass…"

Violet allowed a smile and giggled at Paul's smirk.

"I fell in love with your laugh, with the way you saw the world and that beautiful heart."

"Well, that heart's gone…"

"No your brain-heart. You know what I mean."

Violet brought her hand to Paul's cheek and rubbed his face with her fingertips. Paul laid his hand over hers, pushing her hand closer to his face.

"I don't know how long this will last," Violet said. "That's honestly my deepest fear. Maybe this will be a full life. Maybe it'll be a few years, maybe a month, maybe less..."

"I'll take that chance. maybe this time I'd get a chance to say goodbye."

"Paul—do you really want this?"

"Is it what you want? Deep down?"

Violet nodded.

"Then it's you and me against the world," Paul smiled. "That's all I've ever wanted."

Violet leaned forward and wrapped her arms around Paul. He hugged back, warmth spreading through Violet's body as she buried her face in his chest.

"I missed you so much these last few weeks. When I was alone in the basement, I wanted you to be with me. Every time I fell asleep, I'd hope I would wake up and it would be a bad dream to text you about."

"You can text me about it now," Paul pulled back a little. "Cause I'm not going anywhere."

Rowdy rushed up the stairs and jumped on the bed, licking the tears off Violet's face until both of them smiled. Violet wrapped an around the dog's neck and sighed. "You can come up now, snooper..."

"I wasn't snooping!" Abby said, coming up the stairs. "I was... chaperoning."

"Uh-huh," Paul said, petting the big dog's head. "Just don't go blabbing to everyone at school."

"That the original power couple is back together? You two never let me have any fun! At least I'm back to being your third wheel again and all is right with the universe..."

"And you have to go back to classes, Paul," Violet said, sternly. "Abby can't use the grief excuse anymore, either."

"Wow, you were more fun when you were alive," Paul laughed. Violet wrapped her arms around him again and pushed her face into his collarbone. She could hear his heartbeat in his neck: quick, but steady. Violet could have stayed there forever.

#

Night came slowly, but plans were in place by the time the sun went down. Violet was smuggled out through the garage and into the Greens' family van. Abby sat in the back with her while Benjamin drove, Walter in the passenger seat. Paul stayed a little longer at the end of the cul-de-sac, watching Violet's old house for any signs of her father. His car had left in the afternoon, but no one saw if he had come back. After some time, Violet saw Paul's headlights behind them.

The drive was long, taking a more complicated route in case Violet's father was watching the Greens for any reason. It was paranoia, but Violet had insisted on making sure they were alone. At nearly eleven, they pulled into the motel parking lot and only Paul's headlights followed them.

Shuffling as a unit, the group walked to the third floor room that Violet's mother had indicated. Violet was the one who knocked on the door, tense in the darkness. There was shuffling behind the door, the sound of locks scraping open and the door opened. Before anyone could get a word out, Violet's mother wrapped her arms around her and kissed Violet's forehead. "I was so worried. Come in, everyone…quick!"

Violet and the others rushed in and huddled into the room. The hotel room had two big beds and a chair holding a half empty suitcase open with all of her mother's clothing packed inside. There was a small table with a laptop and Violet's birth certificate and other identification documents for the upcoming court case.

"I took everything with me before I left you father," Violet's mother said. "I figured someone had to take care of your affairs and your father was in no shape to do so."

"So," Abby sat on the bed and crossed her legs. "How does one go about becoming a person again?"

"My concern," Walter said, folding his arms, "is that Violet's father might catch wind of this."

"Tom was always very smart," Violet's mother sighed. "I'd be very surprised if he wasn't already expecting something."

"He's been snooping around the Greens' house already," Violet said. "He's looking around town, but he knows I can't get far on my own."

"Then it's a good thing you're not on your own," Paul smiled, nudging Violet. Violet leaned her head on Paul's shoulder and smiled.

"Alright," Benjamin said, sitting at the table. "We'll start first thing in the morning. I have some documents in my office that might come in useful. And I'll talk to my friend with the missing person's department; I feel like they'll know the procedure to bring people back from legally dead."

"We'll meet tomorrow," Violet's mother said. "I'll go to your office in the morning and we can decide things from there."

"Then we should clear out," Walter clapped his hands together. "It's been a long day for everyone. I'll drive you over to Ben's office in the morning."

"I should get going, too," Paul said. "My mom is freaking out that I'm not home yet."

"I'd prefer if you didn't tell anyone—"

"She thinks I'm jamming at a friend's house tonight. Don't worry, Violet, your secret is safe with me."

"I know," Violet said, wrapping her arms around Paul again. Abby and her parents filed out, eventually taking Paul with them. When they were alone, Violet's mother hugged her again, swaying slightly in the embrace.

"Are you hungry?" Violet's mother asked. "I had some pizza on my way back from the airport, but we could order some room service?"

"I'm just tired," Violet shook her head. "Thanks for letting me stay here. As nice as it was to stay with the Greens, I don't know how much longer I could take the stress. I was worried I'd wake up and be in the basement with…"

Violet lowered her head. Her hands were trembling, but she closed them into tight fists to stop the shaking. Violet's mother held her again and smoothed Violet's hair. Violet suddenly broke down crying. "Why did he do it?" Violet whimpered. "Why didn't he leave me dead?"

"I—your father is a brilliant man, but sometimes that blinds him to the truth. He refused to see the world as black and white. You weren't dead to him, only indisposed. I thought he'd lost touch with reality in his grief, but I didn't think he would become this extreme."

Violet pulled away and sat on the bed, wiping her tears away. Her mother sat beside her, brushing Violet's hair aside. Her fingers traced over one of Violet's facial scars, one of the thicker stitches around her jaw. "Does it hurt?"

"Waking up did," Violet nodded, slowly stopping her shaking. "I don't think I've ever felt so much pain. Now everything else feels numb by comparison."

"Do you still feel everything else? Hot? Cold?"

"Yeah."

"Do you feel this?" Violet's mom asked, poking the palm of Violet's right hand. Violet nodded.

"How about…this?" VIolet's mom asked, a smiling forming as she poked Violet's ribs and made her laugh.

"Don't," Violet smiled a little. "This worked when I was four, it's not gonna work anymore."

"No? I know the back of yours were always ticklish. Maybe that's what it takes to get a smile…"

"Don't you dare!" Violet scooted back as her mother tickled Violet's side. Soon, Violet was rolling on the bed, clutching her sides laughing.

"I can still hear you in your laugh," Violet's mother said when Violet calmed down. "Whatever happened happened, but I will not let anyone hurt you."

After getting ready for bed, Violet took the bed furthest from the door and crawled under the covers. The room was sterile and simple, but Violet wasn't alone for the first time in a while. Violet listened to her mother working on her laptop, answering emails, making requests to attorneys and setting up her appointment with the judge. With the news on in the background, Violet closed her eyes and drifted off to sleep.

#

The car again. The highway. It was easier to tell it was a dream this time. Violet's car was propelling forward, speeding at a set of headlights that never got closer. The hands on the steering wheel were her old hands, but the flickering lights made it look like stitches were raising up between her fingers. The headlights of the truck rushed forward and Violet bolted upright when the truck made impact.

Dull sunlight filled the room. Violet took a minute to control her breathing, a death grip on her sheets. When she felt more relaxed, Violet relaxed her grip and slumped back onto the pillows. The mattress was real. The warmth of the sunlight was real. The air in her lungs was real.

Her mother walked out of the bathroom, straightening out her pantsuit. "Are you alright?"

"Just...collecting myself. I get bad nightmares."

"You've been through a lot, sweetie. I don't think anyone would hold it against you to have some nightmares."

"They aren't...normal nightmares. I can see there's something wrong with my hands. My brain keeps finding things wrong with the dream: my stitches, my eye in the rearview mirror..."

"Rearview?"

"I keep having nightmares of my car wreck. I can usually wake up before the impact, but sometimes I don't wake up fast enough. It's like something in my brain is fighting me."

"You've been through a lot. Be gentle with yourself. Do you want to shower?"

"I would, actually. That sounds great." Violet climbed out of bed and padded barefoot over to the bathroom. When she flipped on the light, her pale skin was whitewashed for a moment while her eyes refocused. Violet turned from her reflection and gripped the doorframe for support.

"Violet? Vi?" Her mother rushed over and took Violet's face in her palms. "Hey, look at me…what's real?"

"The rough of the carpet is real…the smell of soap…the warmth of your hands…" Violet exhaled and slowly blinked twice. "Sorry…most times I'm ready for it, but the mirror snuck up on me."

"Do you want to cover it or…?"

"I have to get used to see all this staring back at me. No amount of bedsheets are gonna undo this."

"Violet, listen to me…" Her mother held her shoulders. "I know this is a lot for you to take in at once, but you've done nothing wrong. You shouldn't be ashamed of what some lunatic did. There is no one at fault here. Now, I'm going down to the courthouse with Benjamin to see about getting our hearing. They're going to want to meet you, but we're still trying to figure out who we even need to call about this."

Violet nodded, hugged her mother again, and slid the bathroom door closed. She looked at her reflection for a bit, testing the full range of her facial muscles and expressions. Turning on the hot water, Violet watched the strange face disappear in a haze of steam. The water on her skin was warm, grounding her in a reality that constantly changed around her.

After her long shower, Violet patted herself dry and went into the hotel room. Changing into some of Abby's spare clothes, Violet found a note stapled to a small, paper bag on her bed.

Violet,

We've told the hotel staff not to clean this room, so you shouldn't have to worry about anyone bothering you today. We thought you'd want a phone to keep in contact. It's not fancy, but it's good enough to text with everyone. We put a few important numbers in there (Me, your mom, Walter and Abby). Walter also insisted on sending a few more books. Humor him and try not to rot your brain with free hotel cable all day? One more thing: Your mom and I will come back around noon with food. Try to stay away from the windows as much as possible. We don't need to tell you to keep the blinds closed for now.

Hang tight and we'll sort this out,

Benjamin

Violet took out the flip phone. It was pretty archaic and frankly she was surprised they had found one this old, but it would be enough for what she needed. All she could do for now was talk to the few people she had. Violet added Paul's number into her phone. She tested the phone by texting Abby:

<<Another long, boring day ahead. Almost makes me miss school.>>

<<You're not missing a lot. But Paul made it to homeroom on time this morning.>>

<<Good. If you see him, tell him I'm proud of him.>>

<<You can tell him later. We're gonna swing by and study during visitation hours.>>

<<Visitation hours?>>

<<Just another step in keeping your identity safe, Betty.>>

<<Ugh, I hate that name. Pick something else.>>

<<Sure thing, Debbie.>>

<<I hate you. See you at 3.>>

Violet set the phone aside. She thought about texting Paul, but decided to let him catch up in class. Maybe over lunch, but for the time being, she wanted him to focus on school. She could get back into his life when she wasn't legally dead. Sitting on the bed, Violet browsed the covers of the books Walter brought her, grimaced at the titles, and set them aside before switching on the TV.

"Any news?" Paul asked, sitting across from Abby. "Yesterday still feels like it didn't happen."

"*Debbie* is still in town, yes," Abby said, sternly looking at Paul over her lunch. "And she's settled into the hotel nicely."

"What are you—? Oh! I see. Have you heard from Debbie this morning, then?"

"Her mom and my dad are reviewing the case, but she sent me a message during first period. She would like us to come see her after school."

"I figured that was a given," Paul said, ripping open his granola bar. "Have you seen her dad?"

"No, but his car was in the driveway when I left for school this morning."

"That's good, right? It means he's not out looking for her."

"Unless he already knows where she is," Abby said. "It's not like we had a lookout last night."

"I was right behind you and I barely kept up. How would he without us noticing?"

"He brought a person back from the dead without anyone noticing. I don't think a little snooping is beyond him."

"Gives me the creeps just thinking about it." Paul shivered, opening his water bottle. "How could someone do that?"

"Grief does strange things. Walter deals with grief patients all the time. They'll come into his office, no idea how they could possibly move on except to deny the obvious."

"Yeah, but I don't think I'd go that far as to bring her back from the dead. I loved her, but I wouldn't even think of bringing her back."

"Dr. Franklin has eighteen awards for excellence in surgery. He's brought people back from the brink of death before. He probably knows more about human anatomy than you or I ever will."

"But this isn't anatomy," Paul shook his head "It's science fiction and nonsense."

"She was sitting with us last night."

"I still can't believe she's back."

"She's here," Abby said, "but who knows if she's back…"

#

By the time 2:30 rolled around, Violet was desperate for company. All the daytime talkshows and free cable gameshows were stale and listless. The books were dull and she didn't want to risk falling asleep to another nightmare. The boredom fueled her paranoia. Anytime she heard footsteps outside her hotel room door, she tensed until the steps faded away. Sometimes, she would get up and look through the peephole, half afraid her father looking back at her.

Violet's mom had come around noon with a grease-stained paper bag of fast food to review their case. The main challenge at the courthouse was proving Violet was Violet.

"We just aren't sure what evidence they'll accept," Benjamin explained over burgers. "If you're up for it, we can have a doctor give you a physical tomorrow after some DNA tests."

"Are we sure that we'll be able to find DNA from when I was alive?"

"You are alive," Violet's mother corrected, "at the very least we can compare your blood type and a few other samples."

After a short lunch and the longer update, Violet's mom and Benjamin took their folder full of documents and went back to the courthouse, preparing to argue their case to the judge. Violet was left alone again and the paranoia only increased until Abby texted that she and Paul were coming.

The knock on the door made Violet jump and she quietly walked over to peer through the peephole. Abby was standing on her tip toes so her face was all Violet could see through the tiny lens. Violet unlocked the door and nearly pulled Abby and Paul into the room.

149

"Thank God you're both here," Violet said, closing the door behind them. "I thought I was going to lose my mind!"

"Not as fun skipping school, huh?" Paul asked.

"It's so boring!" Violet moaned, flopping onto the bed dramatically. "I can't leave, I can't go online, and I can't text either of you during the school day. The only food I've been getting comes in boxes or bags. I'm loath to admit it, but I would kill for an apple!"

"Make us a list," Abby said, sitting across from Violet. "We'll make a supply run for you."

"That'd be great!" Violet sat up. "How about you two? How was school?"

"Uneventful," Paul said, sitting to Violet's side and putting his arm around her. "Still, I felt like a kid on Christmas morning."

The three teens spent the next hour talking and sharing stories. Violet updated them on what her mom and Benjamin had told her, while Abby and Paul explained the things she'd missed during her extended absence. Violet leaned against Paul, eventually laying on the bed with her head on his chest. Paul's hand smoothed her hair and the tips of his fingers would graze her shoulder, tracing the patterns of the stitches. Violet nearly felt like things were normal until his fingers would snag on one of the stitches.

Eventually, Abby and Paul opened their books to do homework, discussing what the classes they had together. Violet was able to chip in what she remembered, but mostly listened to all that she had missed in six months. It seemed like the only thing that hadn't changed was math.

While Abby read for English and Paul worked on his biology homework, Violet curled up against Paul's side with one of Walter's books. The stillness wasn't poisoned with paranoia of worrying she'd be caught. It was the peaceful calm in the small sensations of what she knew was real: pencil scratching on paper, the pages of turning books, the warmth of Paul's hand around her shoulder.

By five, there was another knock on the door followed immediately by the door opening. "Oh good!" Violet's mother said. "You have company! I worry about you being cooped up all day."

"Believe me," Abby said, "a little company goes a long way. And Violet came over after school everyday when I had my wisdom teeth popped out. There's only so much you can do to fill the time."

"I'm just glad I get to see her again," Paul said, resting his forehead on the top of Violet's head.

"Well, I hope you both like pizza. Benjamin is coming back with some, but I'll tell him to bring enough for a couple more."

"How was the courthouse?" Violet asked.

"Good news and bad news," Violet's mother said. "The good news is that the court will hear our case."

"Great!" Abby said, perking up and setting her book aside. "Got to the court quickly!"

"The bad news is that we can't file any charges against Tom until Violet's personhood is reinstated. And Tom is still looking for her. One photograph, one video clip? And Violet loses the luxury of being hidden."

"So, Dad might be able to find me?" Violet asked, paling.

"Benjamin has a restraint request drawn up, but we could just as easily have him arrested if he does anything to hurt us. He'll have plenty of charges against him when we prove what happened, I made an appointment for you tomorrow with a doctor — a real doctor and no one your father knows, I made sure of it."

Violet relaxed. The thought had occurred to her that any doctor in the area would recognize her as Dr. Franklin's daughter. Still, her father had never explained what he'd done, so it would be important to know that she was healthy.

"Can we come?" Abby asked. "Moral support?"

"Sorry," Violet's mother shook her head. "You'll have to be her cheerleader from the sidelines. It's early in the morning and all the tests will take most of the day. I can't make sense of your father's work, but maybe we can get the help of someone who will."

#

Violet was never a morning person. Her mother urged her awake at five in the morning, but Violet only groaned and rolled back over. As Violet's mother made coffee after her shower, Violet rolled out of bed and get ready herself. She showered, dressed and donned her hoodie for the day. Her mother passed her a pair of large sunglasses. They were almost comically large, but they covered most of her face. Sticking her hands in her pockets, she could walk most places without drawing attention to herself.

After an hour of driving to the next town over, Violet and her mom went into the Vanhart Hospital, a six-story building with a large, metal caduceus forged into the brick wall that towered over the entrance. Walking through the parking lot terrified Violet as other people showed up to begin their workday or make their own appointments. Violet knew she was unrecognizable, but she felt as if every eye watched her.

Inside, Violet the sterile stench of the hospital almost sickened Violet. The scratchy audio of the intercom brought back her memories of visiting her dad in the hospital on late shifts. She felt lost in a sea of men and women in white lab coats that Violet felt her father could be hiding in. Violet felt a panic coming, but focused on her feet and the slow, east steps to the elevator. When they got off on the third floor, Violet's mother approached a desk and talked to a young woman with short, blonde hair in an empty waiting room.

"Jane Doe for Dr. DeSantos?"

"Of course," the receptionist said, standing. "We have a room in the back for Miss Doe."

Violet followed her mother and the receptionist to the farthest examination room from the main door. Violet's mother stopped the reception. "I assume, the court briefed Dr. DeSantos about the sensitive nature of this situation?"

"Yes, we've taken every precaution. Jane is safe here, I promise."

Violet the tension in her gut eased long enough for her to comfortably take off her sunglasses. The receptionist flinched, but only instructed Violet to change into a paper gown for the examination. After being weighed and measured, Violet sat on the paper-covered bench and waited for the doctor. As she waited, Violet noted the things in the room that were real: the shine of the metal instruments, the florescent bulbs buzzing overhead, and the smell of rubbing alcohol. There was a knock on the door before the doctor entered.

"Ms...Doe," Dr. DeSantos said. She was an older woman with dark grey hair streaked grey. Her skin was light brown, but wrinkled with age. Her smile was perfectly straight, white teeth and warmer than Violet had expected. If she was surprised, Violet didn't see any change in her face. "I'm Dr. DeSantos. Thank you for trusting me with your examination."

"We just need to know she's healthy," Violet's mother said, her voice breaking for the first time in a while. "We don't know what to look for, but —"

"You want to understand," Dr. DeSantos said, strapping the blood pressure cuff around Violet's upper arm. "I blocked out my whole day for this. I was skeptical at first, but to see it for myself—it would be irresponsible not to ensure you were healthy. How do you feel today, Violet?"

"Sore," Violet admitted, "but that's been pretty typical these days."

"I can't begin to imagine what you're going through. If you'd like, I can recommend a trauma therapist in our building?"

"Let's...just do the physical for now," Violet looked down, unable to look the doctor in the eye.

"Violet?" Dr. DeSantos eased pressure off the cuff. "You don't have to be ashamed of what someone else did to you. Therapy could be extremely helpful, but you can approach that in your own time. But you don't have to hide yourself from me."

"Puts some people off," Violet said, thinking back to the first time Paul or Abby saw her. "Most people who've seen it need a few minutes to recover from shock."

"Most people weren't field medics before becoming doctors. This is a safe space for you. You're going to be treated with the respect you deserve. Now, tell me what you remember of the incident."

Violet recounted everything that had happened to her: the car wreck, waking up in agony in her basement, her confinement, her escape. She didn't always have an answer for Dr. DeSantos, but the doctor took careful notes of Violet's responses. Dr. DeSantos measured Violet's blood pressure, temperature and pulse. She had Violet flex her fingers, do simple exercises, and balance on each leg for as long as she could. Blood, spit and urine were collected and taken for testing in a lab somewhere else in the hospital. Violet was taken down one level where she X-rays taken of most of her body as well as MRI for every inch of Violet's nervous system.

By three in the afternoon, Violet was back in comfortable hoodie and sunglasses. She was exhausted, but stayed while the doctor tried to explain everything. "It will be difficult to know the extent until I've had time to look everything over," Dr. DeSantos said, "and without very invasive surgery, it's hard to know the full extent."

"I've already had an autopsy…" Violet smirked. "How much more invasive can you get?"

Dr. DeSantos grinned a little, but turned serious when she looked at her mother. "For now? I think we can safely say that she won't be in any danger. If she's not in any immediate pain, I think we can assume she's healthy for now, all things considered."

"Thank you," Violet's mother shook the other woman's hand. "We might need to call on your expertise for the court case later. Thank you for believing us."

"I wouldn't have believed it before I saw it myself. I would still recommend a therapist for her...experiences. I can give you the card of our psychologist on the third floor. Tell her to contact me and I can explain the situation."

"Thank you," Violet said, taking the card and shoving it into her hoodie pocket. Heading back through the lobby, Violet was sure that everyone stared at her. She didn't care. All she wanted was to go back to her hotel room and sleep.

In the car, Violet's mother paused in the driver's seat before putting a hand on Violet's fingers. "You did well. You've been doing so well with everything that's been thrown on you. It's not fair, I know. I'm proud of you for being so brave with everything."

"Thanks," Violet squeezed her mother's hand. She leaned over and pushed her head into her mother's shoulder, as close as they could get to a hug with the seatbelt. Her mother started the car and pulled out of the parking lot. By the time they made it back to the hotel room, Abby was waiting for them in the lobby.

"I ran over as soon as school was out," Abby said. "How did everything go?"

"Well enough," Violet said, hugging Abby in the elevator. "Where's Paul?"

"He went to his therapist. Now that things are different, he's got some new things to figure out. I mean, this is a big change from his previous plans, right?"

"Mine, too," Violet said as the elevator doors opened. Back in the safety of the room, Violet told Abby more about the doctor's visit while Abby painted Violet's nails. Violet's mother was typing an email when her cell phone vibrated on the desk. She put on speakerphone and greeted the doctor from earlier.

"I've never seen anything like it," Dr. DeSantos explained. "The technician thought I'd mixed up my samples and wanted a new set, but — frankly I'm not sure where to begin."

"What do you mean?" Violet asked.

"Your blood, for example? It had traces of multiple blood types, different levels of cholesterol in each sample and the hormone levels were all over the place. It essentially looks like it's from different people or a contaminated sample. Your cheek swab? Four different DNA results. Not only that, but there were genetic markers with no obvious correlation to the other inconsistencies. It was beyond a basic mutation."

"So," Violet asked. "What does that mean?"

"There's scientific grounding to your story," Dr. DeSantos said. "I don't know who did this or how, but I think the work they did goes beyond just stitching skin together."

"What about the MRIs?" Violet's mother asked.

"The brain looked very healthy," the doctor continued. "No abnormalities, which is — no offense — very surprising, Your spinal cord is another story. I don't know how, but whoever did this to you must have attached your nerves by hand. A procedure like that would take…days, even weeks, without stopping."

"One questions we want answered above the rest…" Violet's mother swallowed. "Is she going to be alright?"

"Short answer? I think she'll be fine in the long run. There are slight irregularities that might require surgery, but everything appears well from what I can see. The stitching was done with expert care, though it doesn't look like the skin will ever ever fully heal. I think you might have the threading for the rest of your life, without some difficult skin grafts."

"Is that all?" Violet asked.

"Apart from all that? I think you could be mistaken for someone in perfect health."

"That was our primary concern, thank you," Violet's mother said. "Can we call you to the witness stand for our case?"

"I'll offer what I can, but my expertise begins and ends with what I've told you today."

"That's more than any other doctor we could call to the stand," Violet's mother said, taking the phone off speaker and into the bathroom.

"You okay?" Abby asked. "You're doing that...slump you do sometimes."

"I just—I thought this would finally make sense. I wasn't expecting some big 'Oh, we can fix that' resolution, but having a better idea of what will happen would be nice. Will I age? Will the organs fail and need replacing? Can I have kids?"

Abby thought for a minute, rubbing her chin. "Do you want kids? I mean, there are options. There's nothing wrong with adoption."

"I didn't mean it like that!" Violet quickly raised her hand to her forehead. "I mean, I know you're adopted, but with me it was something I'd always thought—shit!"

"Violet, it's okay," Abby laughed. "I know what you meant. You lost something you always felt was in your control. Not having that anymore can be a little disorienting. What I was trying to say is that we can adapt to your new situation. Will you age? Most likely...at least, your brain will. Will the organs fail? I mean...sure, but join the club. Will you ever have kids? If it's what you want, I know you'd move heaven and earth to make it possible."

"You mean that?"

"Ten thousand percent. Whether it's with Paul or someone else, I think you'd make a great mom."

Violet smiled a little and hugged Abby. Abby rubbed her back before pulling away. "And no more of that self-defeatist bullshit, understand? You're gonna have to fight for yourself in court soon enough and I won't be there to convince you how great you are all the time."

Violet nodded and leaned back on the bed. Abby was right. The fight was still to come.

#

The courthouse felt colder than it was outside. The black and white checkerboard floors stretched ahead of Violet, merging with the wooden moulding of the mint green walls. Pale light shined through frosted glass domes suspended from the ceiling, illuminating the way as Violet, her mother and Benjamin all walked through the legal building.

"Do we have to do this in public?" Violet asked. She hadn't been able to wear her hoodie, but compromised with khakis, a long-sleeved shirt and her sunglasses. Still, Violet felt exposed.

"Think of this as a warmup," Benjamin said. "You'll need to get used to people seeing you."

"That's exactly what I'm worried about," Violet groaned.

"It'll be fine," Violet's mother assured her. "I'll be by your side the entire time."

Violet nodded again. She already missed the hotel room and her usual boredom that came with it. Her mother arranged for the hearing as soon as the doctor released the records for us in the court. The judge and the opposing counsel were all eager to see how the case progressed and made the meeting as soon as she could.

When they got to room 115, Violet was relieved to find it looked more like a big conference room than the courtrooms she'd see on television. The long table was arranged with three chairs on either side and a single chair at the end. A big television was attached to the wall with a web camera above the display. There was an abstract print on the opposite wall and a plastic ficus to the right of the door.

Like a lost duckling, Violet sat with her mother while she and Benjamin prepared their notes. The court reporter came in next, a woman in her fifties wearing a dark blue pants suit. Her feathered, blonde hair covered her ears and Violet caught a visible reaction when she made eye contact by mistake. Violet focused down at the table again.

A man in a suit and tie came in next, carrying a black briefcase. His salt and pepper hair was buzzed close to his scalp, making his ears look like they were sticking out sideways. A few pleasantries were exchanged between him and Benjamin. Violet heard him introduce himself as 'Mark Waters' as he shook her mother's hand. Violet looked at him through her sunglasses as he approached, trying to not to be afraid.

"I've heard a great deal about you," Mr. Waters grinned and extended his hand. "I'm representing the State in this case. With any luck, we can resolve this without having to go all the way to court."

Violet swallowed hard, presenting her right hand in his. His face visibly changed when his fingers touched the stitches of her right hand. It wasn't fear or surprise, but more of an amused look, as if he'd discovered a magician's hidden pocket. Violet pulled away and shrank into herself.

"I apologize for staring," Mr. Waters said, walking around to the other side of the table. "I've only heard what Benjamin and your mother had told me, though I didn't believe it."

Violet only nodded and sat down again. Mr. Waters turned to Benjamin with a curious stare. "Can she speak?"

"When I want to," Violet replied, trying to muster some venom into her response. She had died and been brought back to life. She'd be damned if she let this stranger make her feel like she wasn't even in the room. Her hands tensed into fists, but she forced herself to settle as her mother set a hand on her shoulder. The court reporter swore Violet in and the trial began.

#

After the shock of meeting with Mr. Waters had faded, the discussion began. Benjamin and Violet's mom argued that Violet was who she was, brought back to life by unknown forces. Mr. Waters argued that Violet's death certificate was more valid than anything they could offer for proof of identity. At the end of the day, Mr. Waters and Benjamin agreed that a judge would be necessary.

"This was expected," Benjamin said on their way to the parking garage. "We have lots of evidence left to present. If this were an open and shut case, your mother and I wouldn't be so prepared. You did well today, Violet."

"I just want to go back to hotel and hide," Violet set. "That was humiliating…"

"Well, you don't have to worry about going to court tomorrow," Violet's mother said, petting Violet's hair. "The soonest we could get is next week. You've earned your rest."

"I'll let Abby know to meet you at the hotel tonight," Benjamin said. "Or if you'd like, we could get you to the house for a sleepover."

"I think I need some time alone tonight," Violet said. "I'd like Abby's company, but I feel really tired."

"That's fine," Benjamin set a hand on Violet's shoulder. "Tomorrow is Saturday, so we'll all get some rest. I'll have Abby call with breakfast."

Violet forced a smile and nodded. Inside the parking garage, she still felt exposed until she closed the door and was safely in the vehicle. Her mother took her hand and smiled.

"What happens to Dad?" Violet asked. "When we prove everything is true? If he finds out about—"

"One problem at a time. We can't risk interacting with him until we get your rights as a person assured. Benjamin and I can help you figure out what happens later, but for now? Your father isn't here. Nor will he be, if I have any say. I shouldn't have left you with him. If I'd known he was—"

"You couldn't have known. I can still barely believe it."

"Benjamin is already drawing up paperwork to get him arrested, but we need to make sure you're safe first. He's a later problem...much later. Monday? We're taking our case to a judge."

#

Violet spent Saturday with Paul and Abby. Paul brought over his Nintendo and Abby brought movies. It felt like their freshman year when they would hang out in Paul's basement for hours. Violet had nearly forgotten everything else for a minute before her stitches snagged on the joystick of her controller. Paul touched her gently, stole kisses when they were alone, and smoothed her hair when they watched movies.

Sunday passed too quickly. Violet was sure they had been careful, but she and her friends spent the entire day searching for any references of her in the news. Her mother gave Violet use of the computer for the day while Paul and Abby joined her in a conference call.

"Nothing on anything legitimate," Paul announced after an hour of research. "Though I did find a fan fiction for the 'Flesh and Bone' movie franchise..."

"I found that one, too," Violet said. "I'm glad I missed that one if it's anything like the fan fiction..."

"The actual movie is a little less graphic," Abby said. "More brains, less banging..."

"Any sign of my dad?" Violet asked.

"Haven't seen him moving," Abby observed. "But that doesn't mean he's still and quiet."

"Agreed," Paul said. "He was always smart, but paranoid and smart is a lethal combination."

"We've got the paperwork drawn up for restraining orders," Abby said. "Walter has been itching for the police to swing by his house—"

"Until we can prove I'm me or find a trail of bloody bodies to his house, we can't have him arrested."

"We could get a search warrant of the house?" Paul asked. "Try to get the police in there long enough to get him arrested for grave robbing?"

"Right now, all we have is a good story," Abby said. "Benjamin doesn't think it'll be enough to get police involved. Anything out of the ordinary will make Violet's dad suspicious—"

"And it's game over for everyone…" Violet sighed. There was an odd quiet on the conference call and Violet could tell everyone was thinking.

"I'm gonna go check on the dog" Abby said. "I'll call back if I find anything in my research."

Violet was grateful for Abby's sense of timing. She didn't need to tell Paul to stay on the line.

"I wish I could be there right now," Paul said. "In the hotel, in the courthouse…just with you in my arms."

"I still have to go when all this is over."

"Even if we get your dad arrested?"

"There's…there's too much here, Paul. I need the chance to start over…"

"We could—"

"Everywhere I look would be reminders of what used to be," Violet shook her head. "The old neighborhood, school…even the grocery store. And all those people who were at my funeral will see me everyday and—"

"No one will say anything," Paul said.

"They won't need to speak. I can see it people's eyes. The fear that grips them when they look at me. It's the shock on their face when they realize I'm a living, breathing thing."

"That's going to follow you wherever you go."

"It's not strangers, I'm learning not to care about them. If I stay here, I'll need to look into the eyes of people of know. That's the stare that hurts. When you look at me or when I see Abby or my Mom — no, I know, you don't mean it. It takes getting used to. But I need to be somewhere that people won't lament all that I've lost."

"I don't understand, are we breaking up again?"

"No," Violet assured him. "I just need you to understand that I need to adjust to this where people don't know me. I want to meet people and not have their first thought to be 'she was prettier when she was alive' or 'shame what happened' when there's so much more to who I am."

"I understand why you have to leave," Paul said. "It's not about your dad or anyone else. It's about you. I just wish I could hold you like I used to when you were scared. I want to hold your hand and remind you of what's real like we used to. I always told myself it was to keep you calm, but now I know it kept me calm, too."

"When this is over," Violet told him, "we can make this relationship work. After the trial is over and my father is in jail? We can plan the rest from there."

#

At the courthouse, Violet was terrified. She sat in the courtroom next to her mother, waiting with her large sunglasses over her eyes while Mr. Waters settled on his side of the courtroom. The court was all wood panelling with more intricate lights, like flowers hanging down from the ceiling. A heavyset bailiff stood by the door and didn't seem to react when Violet sat at the table with her mother.

The judge was announced by the bailiff and came in as Violet and the other stood up. She had short, black hair and narrow rectangular glasses. She motioned for everyone to sit and looked over the file before addressing the gathered individuals. She flinched, very slightly, but managed to recover well. The judge folded her fingers together and cleared her throat.

"This is the case of Violet Franklin to reinstate her identity," the judge began, "in what I can say is the strangest circumstances that has ever come across my desk. I had to admit that when I first read this, I was… overwhelmed. My medical knowledge and biological expertise are limited."

"We have an expert who can attest to the science, your honor," Benjamin said. "At least, so far as we understand it."

"Do you mean Dr. Franklin?" The judge asked. Violet physically tensed at the thought of her father in the courtroom.

"No, your honor," Violet's mother spoke up. "We'd like to get her identity confirmed and all necessary guardianship transferred solely to myself. We want to keep Violet out of his sight until she is safe, then file charges charges for emotional and physical damages, among other charges."

The judge exhaled and nodded. "I normally would say this is above my scope as a judge, but since this is essentially a case of confirming identity? I think that will be the first problem to solve. Defense, what evidence do you have?"

"We have submitted Violet's birth certificate as evidence," Benjamin handed the first exhibit of evidence to the judge. "As well as the affidavit from Dr. Gloria DeSantos, who has done a full examination of Violet can be brought in as a witness to better explain her physical condition."

"And Mr. Waters?"

"The State submits her death certificate," Mr. Waters announced. "And the expertise of Dr. Tyler Bennet, who performed Violet's autopsy, both in an affidavit and as a witness."

"Very well," the judge said. "While it is unorthodox, I'd like Violet to have an opportunity to speak before opening statements. This is beyond the case of mistaken identity, so I think it is only fair to hear from the accused before we lean into the grueling argument to follow. Violet? Before we begin, is there anything you want to tell the court or myself?"

Violet flinched and stood. Taking off her sunglasses, Violet wrung her shaking hands together until it felt like they would break. She took a final, deep breath and looked up at the judge. "Your Honor," Violet nodded. "I'm still trying to understand everything that happened to me. I have all of the memories of who I was before: playing with my parents, meeting my best friend, falling in love. And I remember dying: the pain that came afterwards and the trauma that no one should have to endure. I feel like I am me. I just want to go live with my mom and go back to my own life, but I can't do that if you don't believe me. I know I'm Violet Franklin. I hope we can prove it. Thank you."

"Thank you, Violet," the judge said. "We'll be handling this with all of the respect and dignity you deserve."

Folding her arms, Violet sat and folded as far into herself as the chair would allow. Her mother squeezed her hand and smiled, rubbing Violet's fingers. The judge nodded, considering Violet's words. With a final exhale, the judge settled into her chair. "Mr. Green? Mrs. Franklin? Your opening remarks, please...."

#

By the end of the day, Violet was exhausted. She figured it was the emotional toll rather than anything she'd had to do. It was an intense, day-long trial where Mr. Waters kept talking about Violet like she wasn't in the room. Dr. DeSantos had given her testimony, explaining everything she had found when examining Violet and lending credit to the story. When he gave his testimony, Dr. Tyler, a lanky, tall morgue technician, looked at Violet as if she was just a propped up corpse, even when she moved. Violet spent most of the trial silently sitting in the chair, protected deep in her sunglasses. By the end of the trial, there was a list of identity trials that Mr. Waters demanded for the next day.

Back at the hotel, Violet fell back into the bed and closed her eyes. Benjamin and her mom were out getting food, but Violet was glad for the time alone. After trying as hard as she did to keep herself from crying, it was nice to finally weep. Wiping her eyes, Violet pulled out her phone and texted Paul.

<<*Today sucks.*>>

<<*Do you want to talk about it? Or should I distract you?*>>

<<*It's been all I can think about all day. I could use a distraction.*>>

<<*Do you remember our first date? That pizza place on Raven Way?*>>

<<*Yeah,*>> Violet laughed a little and poked at her phone. <<*With that guy behind the counter who talked like he was from New York.*>>

<<*Bada Bing, Bada Boom!*>>

<<*Bada Bang!*>> Violet laughed and clutched the phone to her chest. She picked up her device again and wiped her eyes. <<*I think that was the first time I laughed all day.*>>

<<*Should I come over tonight?*>>

<<*No, we're just going to talk court stuff. I don't want to bore you. Besides, I'm gonna just be a weepy mess and you don't want to be around that.*>>

<<*I would only dry your tears, but I understand if you want space. I'll be chilling all night, so text me or call me for more distractions*>>

<<*I love you.*>>

<<*And I will always love you. Have a good night.*>>

Violet closed her phone and rolled onto her side. She cried some more, gripping her pillow tight against her chest. At some point, she'd fallen asleep because she woke up to the sound of Benjamin and her mother coming to the room.

"—fingerprints of five different people," Benjamin said, exhausted. "It puts more credibility to our story, but the fact is that she got more hits saying she was someone else that Waters will just say it proves she's not Violet."

"But we have Violet's birth certificate," Violet's mother said as Violet sat up.

"And the prosecution has her death certificate," Benjamin slumped, exhausted. "We could come up with every legal documents, but we have no physical proof. Fingerprints are useless, her DNA is all mismatched and any identity test will make Waters say Violet is a fraud. I don't know what else we could do at this point."

"What about my teeth?" Violet perked up.

"I'm sorry?" Benjamin asked.

"My skull…" Violet smiled and pointed to her mouth. "My teeth? Dad built the body from the ground up, but was only able to save my brain and skull. Would dental records work?"

"It's a long shot," Benjamin nodded. "When did she last have X-Rays?"

"Her last dentist appointment was…" Violet's mother struggled. "God, March? That would have been a little while before the accident…"

"And she hasn't exactly been abusing her teeth in the time she was dead." Benjamin said. "If we can get X-Rays in the next day or so, that might be enough."

#

"The fillings on this molar," the dentist said, circling the same molar of both x-rays, "and the removal of the back two wisdom teeth make me think these are the same teeth. Additionally, the upper left canines are identical in length and the chip in the lower left incisor are both minute details that would be hard to duplicate. I can confidently say these x-rays, which I took this morning, are identical to the ones we took seven months ago with Violet."

"Thank you, Dr. Marron," Benjamin said. The young man stepped down off the podium and went back to his seat behind Violet and her mother. "Mr. Waters? You've has been asking for physical evidence to prove Violet's identity. Does this satisfy that criteria?"

"I would say yes, but I don't know," Mr. Waters said, genuinely disappointed. "The autopsy done by the morgue technician uses those same records to identify Violet's body on her death certificate. I could use the same X-Rays from seven months ago to confirm the identity of the corpse. I leave this in the court's hands. I won't file an objection, but I don't see a reason why this couldn't be evidence for either side of the case."

The judge took a deep breath and leaned forward, taking off her glasses and rubbing the bridge of her nose. "In most cases of identity, it's simple. We confirm people based on physical evidence, but the…bizarre nature of Violet's circumstances makes this impossible. So, I have to decide what is 'reasonable doubt' in an unreasonable situation."

"Your Honor, wait!"

Violet turned and saw Abby and Paul rushing in, another bailiff chasing them. The judge raised a hand and put her glasses back on. "And you would be?"

"Abby Green: the Defendant's best friend and counsel's daughter—hi, Pop…"

"And you?"

"Paul Monroe," Paul panted. "I'm Violet's boyfriend."

"And you're both here as—?"

"Your Honor," Paul swallowed. "I know Violet better than almost anyone. This person here knows our most intimate secrets…things Violet took to the grave. Things no one would or could fake. I know, in every fiber of my body that this is my Violet. She's had something horrible done to her. Her corpse was defiled and remade, but we're arguing what makes a person!"

"Violet is my best friend," Abby said. "I can't think of a time we haven't been friends. There are things about a person you can't fake. So, we're offering ourselves as witnesses. You can hook us up to any lie detector, make us swear every oath in the book…hell, call a psychic, if you want! But I'll swear on anything that this is my best friend."

Violet looked back to the judge and waited. Tapping her fingers against the desk, the judge considered the situation. "Mr. Waters?" The judge said. "Would the State accept additional testimony?"

"I've never encountered a surprise witness," Mr. Waters said, "but I don't see why we can't take what they say as credible…provided they are willing to go under oath."

"Of course," Abby nodded. "You've been looking at the physical parts of who she is. We can confirm the human parts of Violet."

The judge nodded with a slight smile. "Your surprise witness, defense counsel…"

#

"—isn't how things are done in court!" Benjamin scolded, his hands on his hips while Abby and Paul sat on a bench outside the courtroom. He and Mr. Waters had questioned the two teens for almost two hours before the judge had called a recess to make her decision. "You can't just…run into a courtroom and expect to be heard! If we thought your testimony would have helped—"

"It would have, Pop!" Abby moaned. "You could have sat in there for hours, debating dental records and fingerprints, certificates and legal documents, but that's not who Violet is! We didn't recognize Violet because of her face or fingers, we saw Violet for who she is."

"Well, I hope your little gambit pays off," Benjamin said. "You're both lucky the judge didn't throw you out of court. And don't think this discussion is over, Abby! We'll talk about this with Dad when we get home…and I'm calling your mother, Paul!"

Violet noticed a slight smile when Benjamin shook his head and walked away. Sitting between Paul and Abby, Violet wrapped herself in Abby's arms and hugged her. "You should have told me you were coming…"

"We didn't think we were until about…an hour ago," Abby said. "Next time, pick a closer courthouse."

"But why are you here?" Violet asked.

"Everything we said in there is true," Paul said, putting his heavy arms around Violet and pulling her close. "None of those suits would know you like we did—no offense to your dad, Abby."

"None taken, he is being kind of a suit, at the moment."

"And we couldn't just sit and wait while someone else decided what we already knew," Paul said. "Besides, we're kind of famous for skipping class this year, it's not like anyone will notice."

Violet smiled and pushed her face into Paul's shoulder. Her mother approached and ushered all of them into the courtroom again. "Judge has made a decision."

"Is it good or bad when it takes this long?" Violet asked, holding Paul's hand.

"It means the judge took her time," Violet's mother said, not bothering to sit when they made it to the table. Abby and Paul sat behind Violet, as close as they could get. The judge came in and motioned for everyone to sit down.

"This…is an unusual case," the judge began. "I feel that this could be better handled by philosophers and poets than some earthly judge. What we're asking is what makes a person: the bones and flesh or the thoughts and feelings? I have been considering this while deliberating and decided that it's nothing of these. What makes a person, and what won me over, is our humanity. And Violet's friends and family—here today—have shown me that she has that. So, I rule in favor of the defendant, Violet Franklin. The death certificate shall be voided and she shall be awarded all legal rights that come with that."

Abby's hands wrapped around Violet's shoulders and Violet was smothered in Paul's big hug. Laughing through her tears, Violet grabbed at everyone holding her. When she blinked her tears away, Violet saw the judge's warm smile.

"Miss Franklin? You are free to leave whenever you choose."

"Before we do that, your honor?" Violet's mother spoke up. "We may need you to make another ruling…"

#

Three cop cars filed into Violet's old neighborhood. Eight officers stormed Violet's childhood house while she and her mother watched from behind the line of police cars. After a few tense moments, Violet's father was led out of the house in handcuffs. Violet rushed forward, slipping passed the officers before they could put him in the back of the police car.

"Violet," Dr. Franklin smiled, "I—"

"Whose eye is this?" Violet pointed to her unfamiliar eye. "Who's lungs are these? My heart? Did you even know their names?"

Dr. Franklin stammered for a moment and swallowed. "I kept my notes, yes. Violet, you have to understand, I did what I did because I love you. I knew you weren't really gone…you just needed me to bring you back."

"I didn't ask you to!" Violet yelled. "You kept me in a basement! I felt so hollow and empty! What's the point of bringing me back if you weren't going to let me live a life?"

"I won't lie," Dr. Franklin shook his head. "It was selfish. Violet, no one would have understood why I brought you back. No one can truly understand a father's love."

Violet shook her head, angrily. "I understand perfectly, but I will never forgive you for this. You aren't my father. If your records were that careful, you'd know there's barely any part of me left."

Walking away, Violet heard Dr. Franklin calling after her while the police put him into the car. She went into the old house and walked around, staying out of the police's way. Steeling her nerves, Violet walked down into the basement and watched as police cataloged all the medical tools, photographing and bagging everything they could find as evidence. After a while, Violet couldn't stay in the basement and went up to her old bedroom to collect her things, already boxed and ready to be shipped to her mother's new house.

On her way up to her bedroom, she stopped at her father's old office. A younger forensic officer was taking pictures and bagging Dr. Franklin's computer with plastic gloves on. There was a notebook to the left of the desk that had 'Vi 2' written on the cover.

"Excuse me?" Violet spoke up. "That notebook…is there a list of names in there? Maybe organs next to it?"

The officer grabbed the notebook and flipped through each page. "Yeah," he nodded. "Lungs, heart, stomach—"

"Could you send me a copy of the list? When everything is done, of course."

"This is pretty open and shut," the officer said. "Shouldn't take more than a couple days. If you give me your email, I guess I could send it to you. You are kind of a crucial witness to the case. Why do you need it?"

"Closure," Violet said, watching the notebook get photographed and slid into a plastic bag.

#

Violet's father's trial didn't even go to court. Once he had a lawyer present, he pleaded guilty to all charges. Violet saw the story of Dr. Thomas Franklin's arrest and incarceration on the evening news as she was organizing the last of her possessions to be shipped. The police asked if Violet's mother wanted any of his old belongs that were in evidence, but she only asked for the notebook Violet had indicated.

The old house felt haunted and unsanitary, so Violet and her mother went back to the hotel after sorting through their things. Violet's mother talked with a real estate agent, while Violet went back to the hotel room to start the paperwork to get her driver's license, passport and other legal identification. A uniformed officer delivered the notebook to the hotel later that night. It was the first time Violet had answered a door without knowing exactly who was on the other side.

In total, the list had over a hundred names. Some were entire organs or limbs, but Dr. Franklin had kept a careful list of skin and muscle tissue donations. After reviewing the notebook for an hour, she was relieved when Abby called to come over for morale support.

"There's so much in here..." Abby said, reading Dr. Franklin's quick, messy handwriting. "Not just the names, but he detailed the procedures. He even kept track of dosages of all the drugs he was on to stay awake to reconnect your spine."

"Not just that surgery," Violet said, unscrewing a water bottle cap. "I think he slept once a week in the months he was rebuilding me. Some of this reads like gibberish...the manic ravings of someone out of touch with reality. I can't believe this is the same man who raised me."

"I don't think it was," Abby shook her head. "Grief does things to people. None of us were the same after you died. Your father just...took it to an extreme that no one could have predicted."

"And we're left to pick up the pieces," Violet flopped back onto the bed and sighed. "I have to do something with these names."

"Should we...call the families? Email them?"

"We just have a list of names. No contact information, no way of tracking them down, no hospital of origin...they might all be dead for all I know."

"But you have a plan?"

"Would I be complaining this much if I had an idea?" Violet asked. "I can't find the people I owe my second life to...I just wish they could find me."

"I might have an idea for that," Abby perked up, "but you're gonna have to face your fears..."

"Wanna pull out your ouija board again?"

"I was thinking something with a much longer reach..."

#

Violet finished her paperwork right as Paul texted her that he was there. She stood and opened the door just as he was getting off the elevator. He smiled down the length of the hall as she waited in the doorway for him to come.

"Hey," Paul said, a little nervous. "You sounded serious on the phone. Is everything OK?"

"Yeah," Violet nodded. "I just wanted to show you something."

Paul followed Violet into the hotel room, looking around. "Your mom's not here?"

"Between the real estate agent, the travel agent, the shipping company and the endless calls from reporters, I told her she deserved to take advantage of the hotel's spa. I would have gone myself, but I'm still getting comfortable in short sleeves."

"So, you're still leaving?" Paul asked. "I'd hoped that—"

"I thought so, too," Violet frowned. "Part of me hoped I'd change my mind with my dad in jail, but—"

"You want a fresh start," Paul said. "I get it. And I support it. But to me, you'll always be Violet…my Violet."

Violet shook her head and took his hands. "I'm someone new and I want to explore that…with you, if I can."

"How can I help?"

Violet led Paul to the bed and sat him next to her. She picked up her old laptop and opened the video she'd posted earlier that day. Without saying anything else, Violet played the video. On screen, her face was framed so that all of the scars on her face were visible as well as the difference between the two eyes.

"My name is Violet Franklin," she began in the video, "and I died. You've probably seen the court case or maybe you've heard of my father. Since I was reborn, I've been struggling with my identity and what it means. And that led me to this list. My eye belonged to Bryan Gilden. One of my lungs belongs to Brittany Coleman. And taking all of this in and talking about made me realize that I don't want to start this new life with guilt.

"These parts of me," Violet continued in the video, "were stolen. I can't give them back, but I owe my life to the people who they were taken from. I want to thank them, but I don't know where to start looking. So, I'm posting the list of names. If you know someone on this list, send them this video and message me. It would mean a lot to start this second chance at life with something good."

The video ended and Violet looked at Paul, setting a hand on his shoulder. "It's already been posted," Violet said. "Abby helped me edit it and sent it to a bunch of people from school. Apparently, I made an impression on them. "

"I could have told you that..."

"I'm waiting to hear back from more people, but we already got a few people who are stepping forward. The video is actually circling around a lot. When summer comes around and I'm all caught up on homeschooling and you and Abby are out for the summer, I want to travel around. Abby and I are going to find everyone...learn a little bit about the people who are part of me."

"Why?" Paul asked. "I understand it matters to you, but why not just... thank them and leave it?"

"I need to honor them," Violet said. "I need to know them for more than just pieces of the new me. If I've learned anything because of this? It's that people are more than the sum of their parts. I want to explore that and I want you to come with me."

"Of course," Paul said, wrapping an arm around Violet's shoulder. "I want to be with you...whoever the hell that includes."

Violet wrapped her arms around Paul's shoulder and kissed his cheek. Paul squeezed back and ran his hand over Violet's hair. "I love you, Violet Franklin. And there is nothing that will separate us."

"I love you, Paul Monroe," Violet replied. "And I'm still serious about this long distance thing…you better call me every day."

"For the rest of our days," Paul laughed and squeezing a little tighter.

#

Going through the airport was difficult. Violet was expecting people to stare and her mother had paperwork that supported her story while they were waiting for legal documents to arrive. She was still pulled aside by security, but the security agent recognized her from the news story that had run earlier that morning. A few strangers nearby recognized Violet from her now viral video. Some people even asked for photos.

"To think you wouldn't walk outside a week ago," Violet's mother asked as they sat down for lunch in a small, terminal restaurant. "Now you're posing for pictures?"

"People are gonna stare and take pictures anyway," Violet shrugged. "I might as well smile in them. Smiling feels more me."

"That video was very brave," Violet's mother said. "Do you think you'll be able to find everyone on the list?"

"Honestly? I don't know. I don't expect everyone to contact me, but I'm hoping they hear I'm looking for them and want to thank them."

"I'm proud of you. This hasn't been easy, but you've been so strong for all of this."

"Thanks, Mom," Violet said. "And I think I do want to go to therapy. Finding the list and making the video…those were just parts of the process, but I need help healing. I don't know who I am, but I'm proud of me."

Violet met three more fans while waiting at the gate for her plane. After she took one last picture, the plane started to board. Violet smiled at the flight attendant as she stepped onto the plane. The stewardess's smile broke from a fraction of a second, but Violet could forgive that now. She could only change herself for now, not other people. Violet's mother stopped and motioned for Violet to sit in one of the two, plush seats at the front of the cabin.

"Never flown first class," Violet said to her mother, putting her carry-on above her.

"It's a time for new experiences," Violet's mother smiled. "Besides, I thought you might want a little more comfort for a six hour flight. It's hard enough sitting with some stranger halfway into your seat, so I figured we deserved some privacy."

Violet settled in the window seat and took out her phone. After plugging in her headphones, she got a text from Paul.

<<Back at school today. Everyone is talking about how great you are. You're quite famous.>>

<<As long as I have your affection?>> Violet replied. *<<I don't need the rest.>>*
<<It's gonna be boring without you here.>>
<<I was thinking the same thing. But I could use some boring.>>
<<You're anything but.>>
<<Sap. Flight's gonna take off soon, but I'll text you when we land.>>
<<I'll wait up. You sure you feel good about this?>>

Violet smiled and flexed her hand. The stitching was still rough against her fingertips, but the sensation was familiar now. It was getting that she didn't remember anything besides the tension in her stitching, the hyperawareness of her muscles and the elasticity of her skin. All the things she'd struggled with were becoming second nature again. She sent Paul one final text before turning her phone to airplane mode.

<<I feel more like me than I have in a long time. See you on the other side.>>

Acknowledgements

I would like to thank a number of people for their help with this project.

Devon, Richard and Lacy: Thank you all so much for taking the time to fine tune these stories and getting them cleaned up. After reading them so many times, these stories started to blur. I was relieved to not only get your corrections, but also confirmation that they were actually readable!

Thanks to Emily Congdon for the fantastic cover design! It's absolutely stunning and I love how it turned it. You went above and beyond and I can't thank you enough for the effort you put into this project. Find more of Emily's work at emilycongdon.com

Author Biography

Nicholas Westbrook is a writer and photographer living in Seattle. He is a graduate of Roger Williams University and Southern Connecticut State University with degrees in Creative Writing and Library Science, respectively. He enjoys playing Dungeons & Dragons, should not be left alone in bookstores, and will greet dogs before their owners. More of his writing can be found at www.nwwestbrook-writing.us, where you will also find links to all his social media.

www.ingramcontent.com/pod-product-compliance
Lightning Source LLC
Chambersburg PA
CBHW010639100726
47900CB00011B/2895